The Yellow Wallpaper and Other Stories

Charlotte Perkins Gilman

Charlotte Perkins Gilman

Filiquarian Publishing, LLC is publishing this edition of The Yellow Wallpaper and Other Stories, due to its public domain status.

Filiquarian Publishing, LLC

Contents

Charlotte Perkins Gilman

The Yellow Wallpaper

It is very seldom that mere ordinary people like John and myself secure ancestral halls for the summer.

A colonial mansion, a hereditary estate, I would say a haunted house, and reach the height of romantic felicity--but that would be asking too much of fate!

Still I will proudly declare that there is something queer about it.

Else, why should it be let so cheaply? And why have stood so long untenanted?

John laughs at me, of course, but one expects that in marriage.

John is practical in the extreme. He has no patience with faith, an intense horror of superstition, and he scoffs openly at any talk of things not to be felt and seen and put down in figures.

John is a physician, and PERHAPS--(I would not say it to a living soul, of course, but this is dead paper and a great relief to my mind)--PERHAPS that is one reason I do not get well faster.

You see he does not believe I am sick!

And what can one do?

If a physician of high standing, and one's own husband, assures friends and relatives that there is really nothing the matter with one but temporary nervous depression--a slight hysterical tendency--what is one to do?

My brother is also a physician, and also of high standing, and he says the same thing.

So I take phosphates or phosphites--whichever it is, and tonics, and journeys, and air, and exercise, and am absolutely forbidden to "work" until I am well again.

Personally, I disagree with their ideas.

Personally, I believe that congenial work, with excitement and change, would do me good.

But what is one to do?

I did write for a while in spite of them; but it DOES exhaust me a good deal--having to be so sly about it, or else meet with heavy opposition.

I sometimes fancy that my condition if I had less opposition and more society and stimulus--but John says the very worst thing I can do is to think about my condition, and I confess it always makes me feel bad.

So I will let it alone and talk about the house.

The most beautiful place! It is quite alone, standing well back from the road, quite three miles from the village. It makes me think of English places that you read about, for there are hedges and walls and gates that lock, and lots of separate little houses for the gardeners and people.

There is a DELICIOUS garden! I never saw such a garden-- large and shady, full of box-bordered paths, and lined with long grape-covered arbors with seats under them.

There were greenhouses, too, but they are all broken now.

There was some legal trouble, I believe, something about the heirs and coheirs; anyhow, the place has been empty for years.

That spoils my ghostliness, I am afraid, but I don't care--there is something strange about the house--I can feel it.

I even said so to John one moonlight evening, but he said what I felt was a DRAUGHT, and shut the window.

I get unreasonably angry with John sometimes. I'm sure I never used to be so sensitive. I think it is due to this nervous condition.

But John says if I feel so, I shall neglect proper self-control; so I take pains to control myself--before him, at least, and that makes me very tired.

I don't like our room a bit. I wanted one downstairs that opened on the piazza and had roses all over the window, and such pretty old-fashioned chintz hangings! but John would not hear of it.

He said there was only one window and not room for two beds, and no near room for him if he took another.

He is very careful and loving, and hardly lets me stir without special direction.

I have a schedule prescription for each hour in the day; he takes all care from me, and so I feel basely ungrateful not to value it more.

He said we came here solely on my account, that I was to have perfect rest and all the air I could get. "Your exercise depends on your strength, my dear," said he, "and your food somewhat on your appetite; but air you can absorb all the time." So we took the nursery at the top of the house.

It is a big, airy room, the whole floor nearly, with windows that look all ways, and air and sunshine galore. It was nursery first and then playroom and gymnasium, I should judge; for the windows are barred for little children, and there are rings and things in the walls.

The paint and paper look as if a boys' school had used it. It is stripped off--the paper--in great patches all around the head of my bed, about as far as I can reach, and in a great place on the other side of the room low down. I never saw a worse paper in my life.

One of those sprawling flamboyant patterns committing every artistic sin.

It is dull enough to confuse the eye in following, pronounced enough to constantly irritate and provoke study, and when you follow the lame uncertain curves for a little distance they suddenly commit suicide--plunge off at outrageous angles, destroy themselves in unheard of contradictions.

The color is repellent, almost revolting; a smouldering unclean yellow, strangely faded by the slow-turning sunlight.

It is a dull yet lurid orange in some places, a sickly sulphur tint in others.

No wonder the children hated it! I should hate it myself if I had to live in this room long.

There comes John, and I must put this away,--he hates to have me write a word.

We have been here two weeks, and I haven't felt like writing before, since that first day.

Charlotte Perkins Gilman

I am sitting by the window now, up in this atrocious nursery, and there is nothing to hinder my writing as much as I please, save lack of strength.

John is away all day, and even some nights when his cases are serious.

I am glad my case is not serious!

But these nervous troubles are dreadfully depressing.

John does not know how much I really suffer. He knows there is no REASON to suffer, and that satisfies him.

Of course it is only nervousness. It does weigh on me so not to do my duty in any way!

I meant to be such a help to John, such a real rest and comfort, and here I am a comparative burden already!

Nobody would believe what an effort it is to do what little I am able,--to dress and entertain, and other things.

It is fortunate Mary is so good with the baby. Such a dear baby!

And yet I CANNOT be with him, it makes me so nervous.

I suppose John never was nervous in his life. He laughs at me so about this wall-paper!

At first he meant to repaper the room, but afterwards he said that I was letting it get the better of me, and that nothing was worse for a nervous patient than to give way to such fancies.

He said that after the wall-paper was changed it would be the heavy bedstead, and then the barred windows, and then that gate at the head of the stairs, and so on.

"You know the place is doing you good," he said, "and really, dear, I don't care to renovate the house just for a three months' rental."

"Then do let us go downstairs," I said, "there are such pretty rooms there."

Then he took me in his arms and called me a blessed little goose, and said he would go down to the cellar, if I wished, and have it whitewashed into the bargain.

But he is right enough about the beds and windows and things.

It is an airy and comfortable room as any one need wish, and, of course, I would not be so silly as to make him uncomfortable just for a whim.

I'm really getting quite fond of the big room, all but that horrid paper.

Out of one window I can see the garden, those mysterious deepshaded arbors, the riotous old-fashioned flowers, and bushes and gnarly trees.

Out of another I get a lovely view of the bay and a little private wharf belonging to the estate. There is a beautiful shaded lane that runs down there from the house. I always fancy I see people walking in these numerous paths and arbors, but John has cautioned me not to give way to fancy in the least. He says that with my imaginative power and habit of story-making, a nervous weakness like mine is sure to lead to all manner of excited fancies, and that I ought to use my will and good sense to check the tendency. So I try.

I think sometimes that if I were only well enough to write a little it would relieve the press of ideas and rest me.

But I find I get pretty tired when I try.

It is so discouraging not to have any advice and companionship about my work. When I get really well, John says we will ask Cousin Henry and Julia down for a long visit; but he says he would as soon put fireworks in my pillow-case as to let me have those stimulating people about now.

I wish I could get well faster.

But I must not think about that. This paper looks to me as if it KNEW what a vicious influence it had!

There is a recurrent spot where the pattern lolls like a broken neck and two bulbous eyes stare at you upside down.

I get positively angry with the impertinence of it and the everlastingness. Up and down and sideways they crawl, and those absurd, unblinking eyes are everywhere. There is one place where two breadths didn't match, and the eyes go all up and down the line, one a little higher than the other.

I never saw so much expression in an inanimate thing before, and we all know how much expression they have! I used to lie awake as a child and get more entertainment and terror out of blank walls and plain furniture than most children could find in a toy store.

I remember what a kindly wink the knobs of our big, old bureau used to have, and there was one chair that always seemed like a strong friend.

I used to feel that if any of the other things looked too fierce I could always hop into that chair and be safe.

The furniture in this room is no worse than inharmonious, however, for we had to bring it all from downstairs. I suppose when this was used as a playroom they had to take the nursery things out, and no wonder! I never saw such ravages as the children have made here.

The wall-paper, as I said before, is torn off in spots, and it sticketh closer than a brother--they must have had perseverance as well as hatred.

Then the floor is scratched and gouged and splintered, the plaster itself is dug out here and there, and this great heavy bed which is all we found in the room, looks as if it had been through the wars.

But I don't mind it a bit--only the paper.

There comes John's sister. Such a dear girl as she is, and so careful of me! I must not let her find me writing.

She is a perfect and enthusiastic housekeeper, and hopes for no better profession. I verily believe she thinks it is the writing which made me sick!

But I can write when she is out, and see her a long way off from these windows.

There is one that commands the road, a lovely shaded winding road, and one that just looks off over the country. A lovely country, too, full of great elms and velvet meadows.

This wall-paper has a kind of sub-pattern in a different shade, a particularly irritating one, for you can only see it in certain lights, and not clearly then.

But in the places where it isn't faded and where the sun is just so--I can see a strange, provoking, formless sort of figure, that seems to skulk about behind that silly and conspicuous front design.

There's sister on the stairs!

Well, the Fourth of July is over! The people are gone and I am tired out. John thought it might do me good to see a little company, so we just had mother and Nellie and the children down for a week.

Of course I didn't do a thing. Jennie sees to everything now.

But it tired me all the same.

John says if I don't pick up faster he shall send me to Weir Mitchell in the fall.

But I don't want to go there at all. I had a friend who was in his hands once, and she says he is just like John and my brother, only more so!

Besides, it is such an undertaking to go so far.

I don't feel as if it was worth while to turn my hand over for anything, and I'm getting dreadfully fretful and querulous.

I cry at nothing, and cry most of the time.

Of course I don't when John is here, or anybody else, but when I am alone.

And I am alone a good deal just now. John is kept in town very often by serious cases, and Jennie is good and lets me alone when I want her to.

So I walk a little in the garden or down that lovely lane, sit on the porch under the roses, and lie down up here a good deal.

I'm getting really fond of the room in spite of the wall-paper. Perhaps BECAUSE of the wall-paper.

It dwells in my mind so!

I lie here on this great immovable bed--it is nailed down, I believe--and follow that pattern about by the hour. It is as good as gymnastics, I assure you. I start, we'll say, at the bottom, down in the corner over there where it has not been touched, and I determine for the thousandth time that I WILL follow that pointless pattern to some sort of a conclusion.

I know a little of the principle of design, and I know this thing was not arranged on any laws of radiation, or alternation, or repetition, or symmetry, or anything else that I ever heard of.

It is repeated, of course, by the breadths, but not otherwise.

Looked at in one way each breadth stands alone, the bloated curves and flourishes--a kind of "debased Romanesque" with delirium tremens--go waddling up and down in isolated columns of fatuity.

But, on the other hand, they connect diagonally, and the sprawling outlines run off in great slanting waves of optic horror, like a lot of wallowing seaweeds in full chase.

The whole thing goes horizontally, too, at least it seems so, and I exhaust myself in trying to distinguish the order of its going in that direction.

They have used a horizontal breadth for a frieze, and that adds wonderfully to the confusion.

There is one end of the room where it is almost intact, and there, when the crosslights fade and the low sun shines directly upon it, I can almost fancy radiation after all,--the interminable grotesques seem to form around a common centre and rush off in headlong plunges of equal distraction.

It makes me tired to follow it. I will take a nap I guess.

I don't know why I should write this.

I don't want to.

I don't feel able.

And I know John would think it absurd. But I MUST say what I feel and think in some way--it is such a relief!

But the effort is getting to be greater than the relief.

Half the time now I am awfully lazy, and lie down ever so much.

John says I musn't lose my strength, and has me take cod liver oil and lots of tonics and things, to say nothing of ale and wine and rare meat.

Dear John! He loves me very dearly, and hates to have me sick. I tried to have a real earnest reasonable talk with him the other day, and tell him how I wish he would let me go and make a visit to Cousin Henry and Julia.

But he said I wasn't able to go, nor able to stand it after I got there; and I did not make out a very good case for myself, for I was crying before I had finished.

Charlotte Perkins Gilman

It is getting to be a great effort for me to think straight. Just this nervous weakness I suppose.

And dear John gathered me up in his arms, and just carried me upstairs and laid me on the bed, and sat by me and read to me till it tired my head.

He said I was his darling and his comfort and all he had, and that I must take care of myself for his sake, and keep well.

He says no one but myself can help me out of it, that I must use my will and self-control and not let any silly fancies run away with me.

There's one comfort, the baby is well and happy, and does not have to occupy this nursery with the horrid wall-paper.

If we had not used it, that blessed child would have! What a fortunate escape! Why, I wouldn't have a child of mine, an impressionable little thing, live in such a room for worlds.

I never thought of it before, but it is lucky that John kept me here after all, I can stand it so much easier than a baby, you see.

Of course I never mention it to them any more--I am too wise,--but I keep watch of it all the same.

There are things in that paper that nobody knows but me, or ever will.

Behind that outside pattern the dim shapes get clearer every day.

It is always the same shape, only very numerous.

And it is like a woman stooping down and creeping about behind that pattern. I don't like it a bit. I wonder--I begin to think--I wish John would take me away from here!

It is so hard to talk with John about my case, because he is so wise, and because he loves me so.

But I tried it last night.

It was moonlight. The moon shines in all around just as the sun does.

I hate to see it sometimes, it creeps so slowly, and always comes in by one window or another.

John was asleep and I hated to waken him, so I kept still and watched the moonlight on that undulating wall-paper till I felt creepy.

The faint figure behind seemed to shake the pattern, just as if she wanted to get out.

I got up softly and went to feel and see if the paper DID move, and when I came back John was awake.

"What is it, little girl?" he said. "Don't go walking about like that--you'll get cold."

I though it was a good time to talk, so I told him that I really was not gaining here, and that I wished he would take me away.

"Why darling!" said he, "our lease will be up in three weeks, and I can't see how to leave before.

"The repairs are not done at home, and I cannot possibly leave town just now. Of course if you were in any danger, I could and would, but you really are better, dear, whether you can see it or not. I am a doctor, dear, and I know. You are gaining flesh and color, your appetite is better, I feel really much easier about you."

"I don't weigh a bit more," said I, "nor as much; and my appetite may be better in the evening when you are here, but it is worse in the morning when you are away!"

"Bless her little heart!" said he with a big hug, "she shall be as sick as she pleases! But now let's improve the shining hours by going to sleep, and talk about it in the morning!"

"And you won't go away?" I asked gloomily.

"Why, how can I, dear? It is only three weeks more and then we will take a nice little trip of a few days while Jennie is getting the house ready. Really dear you are better!"

"Better in body perhaps--" I began, and stopped short, for he sat up straight and looked at me with such a stern, reproachful look that I could not say another word.

"My darling," said he, "I beg of you, for my sake and for our child's sake, as well as for your own, that you will never for one instant let that idea enter your mind! There is nothing so dangerous, so fascinating, to a temperament like yours. It is a false and foolish fancy. Can you not trust me as a physician when I tell you so?"

So of course I said no more on that score, and we went to sleep before long. He thought I was asleep first, but I wasn't, and lay there for hours trying to decide whether that front pattern and the back pattern really did move together or separately.

On a pattern like this, by daylight, there is a lack of sequence, a defiance of law, that is a constant irritant to a normal mind.

The color is hideous enough, and unreliable enough, and infuriating enough, but the pattern is torturing.

You think you have mastered it, but just as you get well underway in following, it turns a back-somersault and there you are. It slaps you in the face, knocks you down, and tramples upon you. It is like a bad dream.

The outside pattern is a florid arabesque, reminding one of a fungus. If you can imagine a toadstool in joints, an interminable string of toadstools, budding and sprouting in endless convolutions--why, that is something like it.

That is, sometimes!

There is one marked peculiarity about this paper, a thing nobody seems to notice but myself,and that is that it changes as the light changes.

When the sun shoots in through the east window--I always watch for that first long, straight ray--it changes so quickly that I never can quite believe it.

That is why I watch it always.

By moonlight--the moon shines in all night when there is a moon--I wouldn't know it was the same paper.

At night in any kind of light, in twilight, candle light, lamplight, and worst of all by moonlight, it becomes bars! The outside pattern I mean, and the woman behind it is as plain as can be.

I didn't realize for a long time what the thing was that showed behind, that dim sub-pattern, but now I am quite sure it is a woman.

By daylight she is subdued, quiet. I fancy it is the pattern that keeps her so still. It is so puzzling. It keeps me quiet by the hour.

I lie down ever so much now. John says it is good for me, and to sleep all I can.

Indeed he started the habit by making me lie down for an hour after each meal.

It is a very bad habit I am convinced, for you see I don't sleep.

And that cultivates deceit, for I don't tell them I'm awake--O no!

The fact is I am getting a little afraid of John.

He seems very queer sometimes, and even Jennie has an inexplicable look.

It strikes me occasionally, just as a scientific hypothesis,--that perhaps it is the paper!

I have watched John when he did not know I was looking, and come into the room suddenly on the most innocent excuses, and I've caught him several times LOOKING AT THE PAPER! And Jennie too. I caught Jennie with her hand on it once.

She didn't know I was in the room, and when I asked her in a quiet, a very quiet voice, with the most restrained manner possible, what she was doing with the paper--she turned around as if she had been caught stealing, and looked quite angry-- asked me why I should frighten her so!

Then she said that the paper stained everything it touched, that she had found yellow smooches on all my clothes and John's, and she wished we would be more careful!

Did not that sound innocent? But I know she was studying that pattern, and I am determined that nobody shall find it out but myself!

Life is very much more exciting now than it used to be. You see I have something more to expect, to look forward to, to watch. I really do eat better, and am more quiet than I was.

John is so pleased to see me improve! He laughed a little the other day, and said I seemed to be flourishing in spite of my wall-paper.

I turned it off with a laugh. I had no intention of telling him it was BECAUSE of the wall-paper--he would make fun of me. He might even want to take me away.

I don't want to leave now until I have found it out. There is a week more, and I think that will be enough.

I'm feeling ever so much better! I don't sleep much at night, for it is so interesting to watch developments; but I sleep a good deal in the daytime.

In the daytime it is tiresome and perplexing.

There are always new shoots on the fungus, and new shades of yellow all over it. I cannot keep count of them, though I have tried conscientiously.

It is the strangest yellow, that wall-paper! It makes me think of all the yellow things I ever saw--not beautiful ones like buttercups, but old foul, bad yellow things.

But there is something else about that paper--the smell! I noticed it the moment we came into the room, but with so much air and sun it was not bad. Now we have had a week of fog and rain, and whether the windows are open or not, the smell is here.

It creeps all over the house.

I find it hovering in the dining-room, skulking in the parlor, hiding in the hall, lying in wait for me on the stairs.

It gets into my hair.

Even when I go to ride, if I turn my head suddenly and surprise it--there is that smell!

Such a peculiar odor, too! I have spent hours in trying to analyze it, to find what it smelled like.

It is not bad--at first, and very gentle, but quite the subtlest, most enduring odor I ever met.

In this damp weather it is awful, I wake up in the night and find it hanging over me.

It used to disturb me at first. I thought seriously of burning the house--to reach the smell.

But now I am used to it. The only thing I can think of that it is like is the COLOR of the paper! A yellow smell.

There is a very funny mark on this wall, low down, near the mopboard. A streak that runs round the room. It goes behind every piece of furniture, except the bed, a long, straight, even SMOOCH, as if it had been rubbed over and over.

I wonder how it was done and who did it, and what they did it for. Round and round and round--round and round and round--it makes me dizzy!

I really have discovered something at last.

Through watching so much at night, when it changes so, I have finally found out.

The front pattern DOES move--and no wonder! The woman behind shakes it!

Sometimes I think there are a great many women behind, and sometimes only one, and she crawls around fast, and her crawling shakes it all over.

Then in the very bright spots she keeps still, and in the very shady spots she just takes hold of the bars and shakes them hard.

And she is all the time trying to climb through. But nobody could climb through that pattern--it strangles so; I think that is why it has so many heads.

They get through, and then the pattern strangles them off and turns them upside down, and makes their eyes white!

If those heads were covered or taken off it would not be half so bad.

I think that woman gets out in the daytime!

And I'll tell you why--privately--I've seen her!

I can see her out of every one of my windows!

It is the same woman, I know, for she is always creeping, and most women do not creep by daylight.

I see her on that long road under the trees, creeping along, and when a carriage comes she hides under the blackberry vines.

I don't blame her a bit. It must be very humiliating to be caught creeping by daylight!

I always lock the door when I creep by daylight. I can't do it at night, for I know John would suspect something at once.

And John is so queer now, that I don't want to irritate him. I wish he would take another room! Besides, I don't want anybody to get that woman out at night but myself.

I often wonder if I could see her out of all the windows at once.

But, turn as fast as I can, I can only see out of one at a time.

And though I always see her, she MAY be able to creep faster than I can turn!

I have watched her sometimes away off in the open country, creeping as fast as a cloud shadow in a high wind.

If only that top pattern could be gotten off from the under one! I mean to try it, little by little.

I have found out another funny thing, but I shan't tell it this time! It does not do to trust people too much.

There are only two more days to get this paper off, and I believe John is beginning to notice. I don't like the look in his eyes.

And I heard him ask Jennie a lot of professional questions about me. She had a very good report to give.

She said I slept a good deal in the daytime.

John knows I don't sleep very well at night, for all I'm so quiet!

He asked me all sorts of questions, too, and pretended to be very loving and kind.

As if I couldn't see through him!

Still, I don't wonder he acts so, sleeping under this paper for three months.

It only interests me, but I feel sure John and Jennie are secretly affected by it.

Hurrah! This is the last day, but it is enough. John is to stay in town over night, and won't be out until this evening.

Jennie wanted to sleep with me--the sly thing! but I told her I should undoubtedly rest better for a night all alone.

That was clever, for really I wasn't alone a bit! As soon as it was moonlight and that poor thing began to crawl and shake the pattern, I got up and ran to help her.

I pulled and she shook, I shook and she pulled, and before morning we had peeled off yards of that paper.

A strip about as high as my head and half around the room.

And then when the sun came and that awful pattern began to laugh at me, I declared I would finish it to-day!

We go away to-morrow, and they are moving all my furniture down again to leave things as they were before.

Jennie looked at the wall in amazement, but I told her merrily that I did it out of pure spite at the vicious thing.

She laughed and said she wouldn't mind doing it herself, but I must not get tired.

How she betrayed herself that time!

But I am here, and no person touches this paper but me--not ALIVE!

She tried to get me out of the room--it was too patent! But I said it was so quiet and empty and clean now that I believed I

Chinese Perkins Gilman

would lie down again and sleep all I could; and not to wake me even for dinner--I would call when I woke.

So now she is gone, and the servants are gone, and the things are gone, and there is nothing left but that great bedstead nailed down, with the canvas mattress we found on it.

We shall sleep downstairs to-night, and take the boat home to-morrow.

I quite enjoy the room, now it is bare again.

How those children did tear about here!

This bedstead is fairly gnawed!

But I must get to work.

I have locked the door and thrown the key down into the front path.

I don't want to go out, and I don't want to have anybody come in, till John comes.

I want to astonish him.

I've got a rope up here that even Jennie did not find. If that woman does get out, and tries to get away, I can tie her!

But I forgot I could not reach far without anything to stand on!

This bed will NOT move!

I tried to lift and push it until I was lame, and then I got so angry I bit off a little piece at one corner--but it hurt my teeth.

Then I peeled off all the paper I could reach standing on the floor. It sticks horribly and the pattern just enjoys it! All those strangled heads and bulbous eyes and waddling fungus growths just shriek with derision!

I am getting angry enough to do something desperate. To jump out of the window would be admirable exercise, but the bars are too strong even to try.

Besides I wouldn't do it. Of course not. I know well enough that a step like that is improper and might be misconstrued.

I don't like to LOOK out of the windows even--there are so many of those creeping women, and they creep so fast.

I wonder if they all come out of that wall-paper as I did?

But I am securely fastened now by my well-hidden rope--you don't get ME out in the road there!

I suppose I shall have to get back behind the pattern when it comes night, and that is hard!

It is so pleasant to be out in this great room and creep around as I please!

I don't want to go outside. I won't, even if Jennie asks me to.

For outside you have to creep on the ground, and everything is green instead of yellow.

But here I can creep smoothly on the floor, and my shoulder just fits in that long smooch around the wall, so I cannot lose my way.

Why there's John at the door!

It is no use, young man, you can't open it!

How he does call and pound!

Now he's crying for an axe.

It would be a shame to break down that beautiful door!

"John dear!' said I in the gentlest voice, "the key is down by the front steps, under a plantain leaf!"

That silenced him for a few moments.

Then he said--very quietly indeed, "Open the door, my darling!"

"I can't", said I. "The key is down by the front door under a plantain leaf!"

And then I said it again, several times, very gently and slowly, and said it so often that he had to go and see, and he got it of course, and came in. He stopped short by the door.

"What is the matter?" he cried. "For God's sake, what are you doing!"

I kept on creeping just the same, but I looked at him over my shoulder.

"I've got out at last," said I, "in spite of you and Jane. And I've pulled off most of the paper, so you can't put me back!"

Now why should that man have fainted? But he did, and right across my path by the wall, so that I had to creep over him every time!

Charlotte Perkins Gilman

The Cottagette

"Why not?" said Mr. Mathews "It is far too small for a house, too pretty for a hut, too--unusual--for a cottage."

"Cottagette, by all means," said Lois, seating herself on a porch chair. "But it is larger than it looks, Mr. Mathews. How do you like it, Malda?"

I was delighted with it. More than delighted. Here this tiny shell of fresh unpainted wood peeped out from under the trees, the only house in sight except the distant white specks on far off farms, and the little wandering village in the river-threaded valley. It sat right on the turf,--no road, no path even, and the dark woods shadowed the back windows.

"How about meals?" asked Lois.

"Not two minutes walk," he assured her, and showed us a little furtive path between the trees to the place where meals were furnished.

We discussed and examined and exclaimed, Lois holding her pongee skirts close about her--she needn't have been so careful, there wasn't a speck of dust,--and presently decided to take it.

Never did I know the real joy and peace of living, before that blessed summer at "High Court." It was a mountain place, easy enough to get to, but strangely big and still and far away when you were there.

The working basis of the establishment was an eccentric woman named Caswell, a sort of musical enthusiast, who had a summer school of music and the "higher things." Malicious persons, not able to obtain accommodations there, called the place "High C."

I liked the music very well, and kept my thoughts to myself, both high and low, but "The Cottagette" I loved unreservedly. It was so little and new and clean, smelling only of its fresh-planed boards--they hadn't even stained it.

There was one big room and two little ones in the tiny thing, though from the outside you wouldn't have believed it, it looked so small; but small as it was it harbored a miracle--a real bathroom with water piped from mountain springs. Our windows opened into the green shadiness, the soft brownness, the bird-inhabited quiet flower-starred woods. But in front we looked across whole counties--over a far-off river-into another state. Off and down and away--it was like sitting on the roof of something--something very big.

The grass swept up to the door-step, to the walls--only it wasn't just grass of course, but such a procession of flowers as I had never imagined could grow in one place.

You had to go quite a way through the meadow, wearing your own narrow faintly marked streak in the grass, to reach the town-connecting road below. But in the woods was a little path, clear and wide, by which we went to meals.

For we ate with the highly thoughtful musicians, and highly musical thinkers, in their central boarding-house nearby. They didn't call it a boarding-house, which is neither high nor musical; they called it "The Calceolaria." There was plenty of that growing about, and I didn't mind what they called it so long as the food was good--which it was, and the prices reasonable--which they were.

The people were extremely interesting--some of them at least; and all of them were better than the average of summer boarders.

But if there hadn't been any interesting ones it didn't matter while Ford Mathews was there. He was a newspaper man, or rather an ex-newspaper man, then becoming a writer for magazines, with books ahead.

He had friends at High Court--he liked music--he liked the place--and he liked us. Lois liked him too, as was quite natural. I'm sure I did.

He used to come up evenings and sit on the porch and talk.

He came daytimes and went on long walks with us. He established his workshop in a most attractive little cave not far beyond far beyond us--the country there is full of rocky ledges and hollows, and sometimes asked us over to an afternoon tea, made on a gipsy fire.

Lois was a good deal older than I, but not really old at all, and she didn't look her thirty-five by ten years. I never blamed her for not mentioning it, and I wouldn't have done so, myself, on any account. But I felt that together we made a safe and reasonable household. She played beautifully, and there was a piano in our big room. There were pianos in several other little cottages about--but too far off for any jar of sound. When the wind was right we caught little wafts of music now and then; but mostly it was still--blessedly still, about us. And yet that Calceolaria was only two minutes off--and with raincoats and rubbers we never minded going to it.

We saw a good deal of Ford and I got interested in him, I couldn't help it. He was big. Not extra big in pounds and inches, but a man with big view and a grip--with purpose and real power. He was going to do things. I thought he was doing them now, but he didn't--this was all like cutting steps in the ice-wall, he said. It had to be done, but the road was long ahead. And he took an interest in my work too, which is unusual for a literary man.

Mine wasn't much. I did embroidery and made designs.

It is such pretty work! I like to draw from flowers and leaves and things about me; conventionalize them sometimes, and sometimes paint them just as they are,--in soft silk stitches.

All about up here were the lovely small things I needed; and not only these, but the lovely big things that make one feel so strong and able to do beautiful work.

Here was the friend I lived so happily with, and all this fairy land of sun and shadow, the free immensity of our view, and the dainty comfort of the Cottagette. We never had to think of ordinary things till the soft musical thrill of the Japanese gong stole through the trees, and we trotted off to the Calceolaria.

I think Lois knew before I did.

We were old friends and trusted each other, and she had had experience too.

"Malda," she said, "let us face this thing and be rational." It was a strange thing that Lois should be so rational and yet so musical--but she was, and that was one reason I liked her so much.

"You are beginning to love Ford Mathews--do you know it?"

I said yes, I thought I was.

"Does he love you?"

That I couldn't say. "It is early yet," I told her. "He is a man, he is about thirty I believe, he has seen more of life and probably loved before--it may be nothing more than friendliness with him."

"Do you think it would be a good marriage?" she asked. We had often talked of love and marriage, and Lois had helped me to form my views--hers were very clear and strong.

"Why yes--if he loves me," I said. "He has told me quite a bit about his family, good western farming people, real Americans. He is strong and well--you can read clean living in his eyes and mouth." Ford's eyes were as clear as a girl's, the whites of them were clear. Most men's eyes, when you look at them critically, are not like that. They may look at you very expressively, but when you look at them, just as features, they are not very nice.

I liked his looks, but I liked him better.

So I told her that as far as I knew it would be a good marriage-- if it was one.

"How much do you love him?" she asked.

That I couldn't quite tell,--it was a good deal,--but I didn't think it would kill me to lose him.

"Do you love him enough to do something to win him--to really put yourself out somewhat for that purpose?"

"Why--yes--I think I do. If it was something I approved of. What do you mean?"

Then Lois unfolded her plan. She had been married,--unhappily married, in her youth; that was all over and done with years ago; she had told me about it long since; and she said she did not regret the pain and loss because it had given her experience. She had her maiden name again--and freedom. She was so fond of me she wanted to give me the benefit of her experience--without the pain.

"Men like music," said Lois; "they like sensible talk; they like beauty of course, and all that,--"

"Then they ought to like you!" I interrupted, and, as a matter of fact they did. I knew several who wanted to marry her, but she said "once was enough." I don't think they were "good marriages" though.

"Don't be foolish, child," said Lois, "this is serious. What they care for most after all is domesticity. Of course they'll fall in love with anything; but what they want to marry is a homemaker. Now we are living here in an idyllic sort of way, quite conducive to falling in love, but no temptation to marriage. If I were you--if I really loved this man and wished to marry him, I would make a home of this place."

"Make a home?--why it is a home. I never was so happy anywhere in my life. What on earth do you mean, Lois?"

"A person might be happy in a balloon, I suppose," she replied, "but it wouldn't be a home. He comes here and sits talking with us, and it's quiet and feminine and attractive--and then we hear that big gong at the Calceolaria, and off we go stopping through the wet woods--and the spell is broken. Now you can cook." I could cook. I could cook excellently. My esteemed Mama had rigorously taught me every branch of what is now called "domestic science;" and I had no objection to the work, except that it prevented my doing anything else. And one's hands are not so nice when one cooks and washes dishes,--I need nice hands for my needlework. But if it was a question of pleasing Ford Mathews--

Lois went on calmly. "Miss Caswell would put on a kitchen for us in a minute, she said she would, you know, when we took the cottage. Plenty of people keep house up here,--we, can if we want to."

"But we don't want to," I said, "we never have wanted to. The very beauty of the place is that it never had any house-keeping about it. Still, as you say, it would be cosy on a wet night, we could have delicious little suppers, and have him stay--"

"He told me he had never known a home since he was eighteen," said Lois.

That was how we came to install a kitchen in the Cottagette. The men put it up in a few days, just a lean-to with a window, a sink and two doors. I did the cooking. We had nice things, there is no denying that; good fresh milk and vegetables particularly, fruit is hard to get in the country, and meat too, still we managed nicely; the less you have the more you have to manage--it takes time and brains, that's all.

Lois likes to do housework, but it spoils her hands for practicing, so she can't; and I was perfectly willing to do it--it was all in the interest of my own heart. Ford certainly enjoyed it. He dropped in often, and ate things with undeniable relish. So I was pleased, though it did interfere with my work a good deal. I always work best in the morning; but of course housework has to be done in the morning too; and it is astonishing how much work there is in the littlest kitchen. You go in for a minute, and you see this thing and that thing and the other thing to be done, and your minute is an hour before you know it.

When I was ready to sit down the freshness of the morning was gone somehow. Before, when I woke up, there was only the clean wood smell of the house, and then the blessed out-of-doors: now I always felt the call of the kitchen as soon as I woke. An oil stove will smell a little, either in or out of the house; and soap, and--well you know if you cook in a bedroom how it makes the room feel differently? Our house had been only bedroom and parlor before.

We baked too--the baker's bread was really pretty poor, and Ford did enjoy my whole wheat, and brown, and especially hot rolls and gems. it was a pleasure to feed him, but it did heat up the house, and me. I never could work much--at my work--baking days. Then, when I did get to work, the people would come with things,--milk or meat or vegetables, or children with berries; and what distressed me most was the wheelmarks on our meadow. They soon made quite a road--they had to of course, but I hated it--I lost that lovely sense of being on the last edge and looking over--we were just a bead on a string like other houses. But it was quite true that I loved this man, and would do more than this to please him. We couldn't go off so freely on excursions as we used, either; when meals are to be prepared someone has to be there, and to take in things when they come. Sometimes Lois stayed in, she always asked to, but mostly I did. I couldn't let her spoil her summer on my account. And Ford certainly liked it.

He came so often that Lois said she thought it would look better if we had an older person with us; and that her mother could come if I wanted her, and she could help with the work of course. That seemed reasonable, and she came. I wasn't very fond of Lois's mother, Mrs. Fowler, but it did seem a little conspicuous, Mr. Mathews eating with us more than he did at the Calceolaria.

There were others of course, plenty of them dropping in, but I didn't encourage it much, it made so much more work. They would come in to supper, and then we would have musical evenings. They offered to help me wash dishes, some of them, but a new hand in the kitchen is not much help, I preferred to do it myself; then I knew where the dishes were.

Ford never seemed to want to wipe dishes; though I often wished he would.

So Mrs. Fowler came. She and Lois had one room, they had to,--and she really did a lot of the work, she was a very practical old lady.

Then the house began to be noisy. You hear another person in a kitchen more than you hear yourself, I think,--and the walls were only boards. She swept more than we did too. I don't think much sweeping is needed in a clean place like that; and she dusted all the time; which I know is unnecessary. I still did most of the cooking, but I could get off more to draw, out-of-doors; and to walk. Ford was in and out continually, and, it seemed to me, was really coming nearer. What was one summer of interrupted work, of noise and dirt and smell and constant meditation on what to eat next, compared to a lifetime of love? Besides--if he married me--I should have to do it always, and might as well get used to it.

Lois kept me contented, too, telling me nice things that Ford said about my cooking. "He does appreciate it so," she said.

One day he came around early and asked me to go up Hugh's Peak with him. It was a lovely climb and took all day. I demurred a little, it was Monday, Mrs. Fowler thought it was cheaper to have a woman come and wash, and we did, but it certainly made more work.

"Never mind," he said, "what's washing day or ironing day or any of that old foolishness to us? This is walking day--that's what it is." It was really, cool and sweet and fresh,--it had rained in the night,--and brilliantly clear.

"Come along!" he said. "We can see as far as Patch Mountain I'm sure. There'll never be a better day."

"Is anyone else going?" I asked.

"Not a soul. It's just us. Come."

I came gladly, only suggesting--"Wait, let me put up a lunch."

"I'll wait just long enough for you to put on knickers and a short skirt," said he. "The lunch is all in the basket on my back. I know how long it takes for you women to 'put up' sandwiches and things."

We were off in ten minutes, light-footed and happy, and the day was all that could be asked. He brought a perfect lunch, too, and had made it all himself. I confess it tasted better to me than my own cooking; but perhaps that was the climb.

When we were nearly down we stopped by a spring on a broad ledge, and supped, making tea as he liked to do out-of-doors. We saw the round sun setting at one end of a world view, and the round moon rising at the other; calmly shining each on each.

And then he asked me to be his wife.--

We were very happy.

"But there's a condition!" said he all at once, sitting up straight and looking very fierce. "You mustn't cook!"

"What!" said I. "Mustn't cook?"

"No," said he, "you must give it up--for my sake."

I stared at him dumbly.

"Yes, I know all about it," he went on, "Lois told me. I've seen a good deal of Lois--since you've taken to cooking. And since I would talk about you, naturally I learned a lot. She told me how you were brought up, and how strong your domestic instincts were--but bless your artist soul dear girl, you have some others!" Then he smiled rather queerly and murmured, "surely in vain the net is spread in the sight of any bird."

"I've watched you, dear, all summer;" he went on, "it doesn't agree with you.

"Of course the things taste good--but so do my things! I'm a good cook myself. My father was a cook, for years--at good wages. I'm used to it you see.

"One summer when I was hard up I cooked for a living--and saved money instead of starving."

"O ho!" said I, "that accounts for the tea--and the lunch!"

"And lots of other things," said he. "But you haven't done half as much of your lovely work since you started this kitchen business, and--you'll forgive me, dear--it hasn't been as good. Your work is quite too good to lose; it is a beautiful and distinctive art, and I don't want you to let it go. What would you think of me if I gave up my hard long years of writing for the easy competence of a well-paid cook!"

I was still too happy to think very clearly. I just sat and looked at him. "But you want to marry me?" I said.

"I want to marry you, Malda,--because I love you--because you are young and strong and beautiful--because you are wild and sweet and--fragrant, and--elusive, like the wild flowers you love. Because you are so truly an artist in your special way, seeing beauty and giving it to others. I love you because of all this, because you are rational and highminded and capable of friendship,--and in spite of your cooking!"

"But--how do you want to live?"

"As we did here--at first," he said. "There was peace, exquisite silence. There was beauty--nothing but beauty. There were the clean wood odors and flowers and fragrances and sweet wild wind. And there was you--your fair self, always delicately dressed, with white firm fingers sure of touch in delicate true work. I loved you then. When you took to cooking it jarred on me. I have been a cook, I tell you, and I know what it is. I hated it--to see my wood-flower in a kitchen. But Lois told me about how you were brought up to it and loved it--and I said to myself, 'I love this woman; I will wait and see if I love her even as a cook.' And I do, Darling: I withdraw the condition. I will love you always, even if you insist on being my cook for life!"

"O I don't insist!" I cried. "I don't want to cook--I want to draw! But I thought--Lois said--How she has misunderstood you!"

"It is not true, always, my dear," said he, "that the way to a man's heart is through his stomach; at least it's not the only way. Lois doesn't know everything, she is young yet! And perhaps for my sake you can give it up. Can you sweet?"

Could I? Could I? Was there ever a man like this?

A Coincidence

"O that! It was a fortunate coincidence, wasn't it? All things work together for good with those who love the Lord, you know, and Emma Ordway is the most outrageously Christian woman I ever knew. It did look that Autumn as if there was no way out of it, but things do happen, sometimes.

I dropped in rather late one afternoon to have a cup of tea with Emma, hoping against hope that Mirabella Vlack wouldn't be on hand; but she was, of course, and gobbling. There never was such a woman for candy and all manner of sweet stuff. I can remember her at school, with those large innocent eyes, and that wide mouth, eating Emma's nicest tidbits even then.

Emma loves sweets but she loves her friends better, and never gets anything for herself unless there is more than enough for everybody. She is very fond of a particular kind of fudge I make, has been fond of it for thirty years, and I love to make it for her once in a while, but after Mirabella came--I might as well have made it for her to begin with.

I devised the idea of bringing it in separate boxes, one for each, but bless you! Mirabella kept hers in her room, and ate Emma's!

"O I've left mine up stairs!" she'd say; "Let me go up and get it;"--and of course Emma wouldn't hear of such a thing. Trust Emma!

I've loved that girl ever since she was a girl, in spite of her preternatural unselfishness. And I've always hated those Vlack girls, both of them, Mirabella the most. At least I think so when I'm with her. When I'm with Arabella I'm not so sure. She married a man named Sibthorpe, just rich.

They were both there that afternoon, the Vlack girls I mean, and disagreeing as usual. Arabella was lean and hard and rigorously well dressed, she meant to have her way in this world and generally got it. Mirabella was thick and soft. Her face was draped puffily upon its unseen bones, and of an unwholesome color because of indigestion. She was the type that suggests cushioned upholstery, whereas Arabella's construction was evident.

"You don't look well, Mirabella," said she.

"I am well," replied her sister, "Quite well I assure you."

Mirabella was at that time some kind of a holy thoughtist. She had tried every variety of doctor, keeping them only as long as they did not charge too much, and let her eat what she pleased; which necessitated frequent change.

Mrs. Montrose smiled diplomatically, remarking "What a comfort these wonderful new faiths are!" She was one of Emma's old friends, and was urging her to go out to California with them and spend the winter. She dilated on the heavenly beauty and sweetness of the place till it almost made my mouth water, and Emma!--she loved travel better than anything, and California was one of the few places she had not seen.

Then that Vlack girl began to perform. "Why don't you go, Emma?" she said. "I'm not able to travel myself," (she wouldn't admit she was pointedly left out), "but that's no reason you should miss such a delightful opportunity. I can be housekeeper for you in your absence." This proposition had been tried once. All Emma's old servants left, and she had to come back in the middle of her trip, and re-organize the household.

Thus Mirabella, looking saintly and cheerful. And Emma--I could have shaken her soundly where she sat--Emma smiled bravely at Mrs. Montrose and thanked her warmly; she'd love it above all things, but there were many reasons why she couldn't leave home that winter. And we both knew there was only one, a huge thing in petticoats sitting gobbling there.

One or two other old friends dropped in, but they didn't stay long; they never did any more, and hardly any men came now. As I sat there drinking my pale tea I heard these people asking Emma why she didn't do this any more, and why she didn't come to that any more, and Emma just as dignified and nice as you please, telling all sorts of perforated paper fibs to explain and decline. One can't be perfect, and nobody could be as absolutely kind and gracious and universally beloved as Emma if she always told the plain truth.

I'd brought in my last protege that day, Dr. Lucy Barnes, a small quaint person, with more knowledge of her profession than her looks would indicate. She was a very wise little creature altogether. I had been studying chemistry with her, just for fun. You never know when yon may want to know a thing.

It was fine to see Dr. Lucy put her finger on Mirabella's weakness.

There that great cuckoo sat and discoursed on the symptoms she used to have, and would have now if it wasn't for "science"; and there I sat and watched Emma, and I declare she seemed to age visibly before my eyes.

Was I to keep quiet and let one of the nicest women that ever breathed be worn into her grave by that--Incubus? Even if she hadn't been a friend of mine, even if she hadn't been too good for this world, it would have been a shame. As it was the outrage cried to heaven.--and nobody could do anything.

Here was Emma, a widow, and in her own house; you couldn't coerce her. And she could afford it, as far as money went, you couldn't interfere that way. She had been so happy! She'd got over being a widow--I mean got used to it, and was finding her own feet. Her children were all married and reasonably happy, except the youngest, who was unreasonably happy; but time would make that all right. The Emma really began to enjoy life. Her health was good; she'd kept her looks wonderfully; and all the vivid interests of her girlhood cropped up again. She began to study things; to go to lectures and courses of lectures; to travel every year to a new place; to see her old friends and make new ones. She never liked to keep house, but Emma was so idiotically unselfish that she never would enjoy herself as long as there was anybody at home to give up to.

And then came Mirabella Vlack.

She came for a visit, at least she called one day with her air of saintly patience, and a miserable story of her loneliness and unhappiness, and how she couldn't bear to be dependent on Arabella--Arabella was so unsympathetic!--and that misguided Emma invited her to visit her for awhile.

That was five years ago. Five years! And here she sat, gobbling, forty pounds fatter and the soul of amiability, while Emma grew old.

Of course we all remonstrated--after it was too late.

Emma had a right to her own visitors--nobody ever dreamed that the thing was permanent, and nobody could break down that adamantine wall of Christian virtue she suffered behind, not owning that she suffered.

It was a problem.

But I love problems, human problems, better even than problems in chemistry, and they are fascinating enough.

First I tried Arabella. She said she regretted that poor Mirabella would not come to her loving arms. You see Mirabella had tried them, for about a year after her husband died, and preferred Emma's.

"It really doesn't look well," said Arabella. "Here am I alone in these great halls, and there is my only sister preferring to live with a comparative stranger! Her duty is to live with me, where I can take care of her."

Not much progress here. Mirabella did not want to be taken care of by a fault-finding older sister--not while Emma was in reach. It paid, too. Her insurance money kept her in clothes, and she could save a good deal, having no living expenses. As long as she preferred living with Emma Ordway, and Emma let her--what could anybody do?

It was getting well along in November, miserable weather.

Emma had a cough that hung on for weeks and weeks, she couldn't seem to gather herself together and throw it off, and Mirabella all the time assuring her that she had no cough at all!

Certain things began to seem very clear to me.

One was the duty of a sister, of two sisters. One was the need of a change of climate for my Emma.

One was that ever opening field of human possibilities which it has been the increasing joy of my lifetime to study.

I carried two boxes of my delectable fudge to those ladies quite regularly, a plain white one for Emma, a pretty colored one for the Incubus.

"Are you sure it is good for you?" I asked Mirabella; "I love to make it and have it appreciated, but does your Doctor think it is good for you?"

Strong in her latest faith she proudly declared she could eat anything. She could--visibly. So she took me up short on this point, and ate several to demonstrate immunity--out of Emma's box.

Nevertheless, in spite of all demonstration she seemed to grow somewhat--queasy--shall we say? --and drove poor Emma almost to tears trying to please her in the matter of meals.

Then I began to take them both out to ride in my motor, and to call quite frequently on Arabella; they couldn't well help it, you see, when I stopped the car and hopped out. "Mrs. Sibthorpe's sister" I'd always say to the butler or maid, and she'd always act as if she owned the house--that is if Arabella was out.

Then I had a good talk with Emma's old doctor, and he quite frightened her.

"You ought to close up the house," he said, "and spend the winter in a warm climate. You need complete rest and change, for a long time, a year at least," he told her. I urged her to go.

"Do make a change," I begged. "Here's Mrs. Sibthorpe perfectly willing to keep Mirabella--she'd be just as well off there; and you do really need a rest."

Emma smiled that saintly smile of hers, and said, "Of course, if Mirabella would go to her sister's awhile I could leave? But I can't ask her to go."

I could. I did. I put it to her fair and square,--the state of Emma's health, her real need to break up housekeeping, and how Arabella was just waiting for her to come there. But what's the use of talking to that kind? Emma wasn't sick, couldn't be sick, nobody could. At that very moment she paused suddenly, laid a fat hand on a fat side with an expression that certainly looked like pain; but she changed it for one of lofty and determined faith, and seemed to feel better. It made her cross though, as near it as she ever gets. She'd have been rude I think, but she likes my motor, to say nothing of my fudge.

I took them both out to ride that very afternoon, and Dr. Lucy with us.

Emma, foolish thing, insisted on sitting with the driver, and Mirabella made for her pet corner at once. I put Dr. Lucy in the middle, and encouraged Mirabella in her favorite backsliding, the discussion of her symptoms--the symptoms she used to have--or would have now if she gave way to "error."

Dr. Lucy was ingeniously sympathetic. She made no pretence of taking up the new view, but was perfectly polite about it.

"Judging from what you tell me", she said, "and from my own point of view, I should say that you had a quite serious digestive trouble; that you had a good deal of pain now and then; and were quite likely to have a sudden and perhaps serious attack. But that is all nonsense to you I suppose."

"Of course it is!" said Mirabella, turning a shade paler.

We were running smoothly down the to avenue where Arabella lived.

"Here's something to cheer you up," I said, producing my two boxes of fudge. One I passed around in front to Emma; she couldn't share it with us. The other I gave Mirabella.

She fell upon it at once; perfunctorily offering some to Dr. Lucy, who declined; and to me. I took one for politeness's sake, and casually put it in my pocket.

We had just about reached Mrs. Sibthorpe's gate when Mirabella gave in.

"Oh I have such a terrible pain!" said she. "Oh Dr. Lucy! What shall I do?"

"Shall I take you down to your healer?" I suggested; but Mirabella was feeling very badly indeed.

"I think I'd better go in here a moment," she said; and in five minutes we had her in bed in what used to be her room.

Dr. Lucy seemed averse to prescribe.

"I have no right to interfere with your faith, Mrs. Vlack," she said. "I have medicines which I think would relieve you, but you do not believe in them. I think you should summon your--practitioner, at once."

"Oh Dr. Lucy!" gasped poor Mirabella, whose aspect was that of a small boy in an August orchard. "Don't leave me! Oh do something for me quick!"

"Will you do just what I say?"

"I will! I will; I'll do anything!" said Mirabella, curling up in as small a heap as was possible to her proportions, and Dr. Lucy took the case.

We waited in the big bald parlors till she came down to tell us what was wrong. Emma seemed very anxious, but then Emma is a preternatural saint.

Arabella came home and made a great todo. "So fortunate that she was near my door!" she said. "Oh my poor sister! I am so glad she has a real doctor!"

The real doctor came down after a while. "She is practically out of pain," she said, "and resting quietly. But she is extremely weak, and ought not to be moved for a long time."

"She shall not be!" said Arabella fervently. "My own sister! I am so thankful she came to me in her hour of need!"

I took Emma away. "Let's pick up Mrs. Montrose," I said. "She's tired out with packing--the air will do her good."

She was glad to come. We all sat back comfortably in the big seat and had a fine ride; and then Mrs. Montrose had us both come in and take dinner with her. Emma ate better than I'd seen her in months, and before she went home it was settled that she leave with Mrs. Montrose on Tuesday.

Dear Emma! She was as pleased as a child. I ran about with her, doing a little shopping. "Don't bother with anything," I said, "You can get things out there. Maybe you'll go on to Japan next spring with the James's."

"If we could sell the house I would!" said Emma. She brisked and sparkled--the years fell off from her--she started off looking fairly girlish in her hope and enthusiasm.

I drew a long sigh of relief.

Mr. MacAvelly has some real estate interests.

The house was sold before Mirabella was out of bed.

Charlotte Perkins Gilman

Making a Living

"There won't be any litigation and chicanery to help you out, young man. I've fixed that. Here are the title deeds of your precious country-place; you can sit in that hand-made hut of yours and make poetry and crazy inventions the rest of your life! The water's good--and I guess you can live on the chestnuts!"

"Yes, sir," said Arnold Blake, rubbing his long chin dubiously. "I guess I can."

His father surveyed him with entire disgust. "If you had wit enough you might rebuild that old saw-mill and make a living off it!"

"Yes, sir," said Arnold again. "I had thought of that."

"You had, had you?" sneered his father. "Thought of it because it rhymed, I bet you! Hill and mill, eh? Hut and nut, trees and breeze, waterfall--beat-'em-all? I'm something of a poet myself, you see! Well,--there's your property. And with what your

Mother left you will buy books and writing paper! As for my property--that's going to Jack. I've got the papers for that too. Not being an idiot I've saved out enough for myself--no Lear business for mine! Well, boy--I'm sorry you're a fool. But you've got what you seem to like best."

"Yes, sir," said Arnold once more. "I have, and I'm really much obliged to you, Father, for not trying to make me take the business."

Then young John Blake, pattern and image of his father, came into possession of large assets and began to use them in the only correct way; to increase and multiply without end.

Then old John Blake, gazing with pride on his younger son, whose acumen almost compensated him for the bitter disappointment of being father to a poet; set forth for a season of rest and change.

"I'm going to see the world! I never had time before!" quoth he; and started off for Europe, Asia, and Africa.

Then Arnold Blake, whose eyes were the eyes of a poet, but whose mouth had a touch of resemblance to his father's, betook himself to his Hill.

But the night before they separated, he and his brother both proposed to Ella Sutherland. John because he had made up his mind that it was the proper time for him to marry, and this was the proper woman; and Arnold because he couldn't help it.

John got to work first. He was really very fond of Ella, and made hot love to her. It was a painful surprise to him to be refused. He argued with her. He told her how much he loved her.

"There are others!" said Miss Ella.

He told her how rich he was.

"That isn't the point," said Ella.

He told her how rich he was going to be.

"I'm not for sale!" said Ella, "even on futures!"

Then he got angry and criticised her judgement.

"It's a pity, isn't it," she said, "for me to have such poor judgment--and for you to have to abide by it!"

"I won't take your decision," said John. "You're only a child yet. In two years' time you'll be wiser. I'll ask you again then."

"All right," said Ella. "I'll answer you again then."

John went away, angry, but determined.

Arnold was less categorical.

"I've no right to say a word," he began, and then said it. Mostly he dilated on her beauty and goodness and his overmastering affection for her.

"Are you offering marriage?" she inquired, rather quizzically.

"Why yes--of course!" said he, "only--only I've nothing to offer."

"There's you!" said Ella.

"But that's so little!" said Arnold. "O! if you will wait for me!--I will work!--"

"What will you work at?" said Ella.

Arnold laughed. Ella laughed. "I love to camp out!" said she.

"Will you wait for me a year?" said Arnold.

"Ye-es," said Ella. I'll even wait two--if I have to. But no longer!"

"What will you do then?" asked Arnold miserably.

"Marry you," said Ella.

So Arnold went off to his Hill.

What was one hill among so many? There they arose about him, far green, farther blue, farthest purple, rolling away to the real peaks of the Catskills. This one had been part of his mother's father's land; a big stretch, coming down to them from an old Dutch grant. It ran out like a promontory into the winding valley below; the valley that had been a real river when the Catskills were real mountains. There was some river there yet, a little sulky stream, fretting most of the year in its sunken stony bed, and losing its temper altogether when the spring floods came.

Arnold did not care much for the river--he had a brook of his own; an ideal brook, beginning with an over-flowing spring; and giving him three waterfalls and a lake on his own land. It was a very little lake and handmade. In one place his brook ran through a narrow valley or valleyette--so small it was; and a few weeks of sturdy work had damned the exit and made a lovely pool. Arnold did that years ago, when he was a great hulking brooding boy, and used to come up there with his mother in summer; while his father stuck to the office and John went to Bar Harbor with his chums. Arnold could work hard even if he was a poet.

He quarried stone from his hill--as everyone did in those regions; and built a small solid house, adding to it from year to year; that was a growing joy as long as the dear mother lived.

This was high up, near the dark, clear pool of the spring; he had piped the water into the house--for his mother's comfort. It stood on a level terrace, fronting south-westward; and every season he did more to make it lovely. There was a fine smooth lawn there now and flowering vines and bushes; every pretty wild thing that would grow and bloom of itself in that region, he collected about him.

That dear mother had delighted in all the plants and trees; she studied about them and made observations, while he enjoyed them--and made poems.

The chestnuts were their common pride. This hill stood out among all the others in the flowering time, like a great pompon, and the odor of it was by no means attractive--unless you happened to like it, as they did.

The chestnut crop was tremendous; and when Arnold found that not only neighboring boys, but business expeditions from the city made a practice of rifling his mountain garden, he raged for one season and acted the next. When the first frost dropped the great burrs, he was on hand, with a posse of strong young fellows from the farms about. They beat and shook and harvested, and sack upon sack of glossy brown nuts were piled on wagons and sent to market by the owner instead of the depredator.

Then he and his mother made great plans, the eager boy full of ambition. He studied forestry and arboriculture; and grafted the big fat foreign chestnut on his sturdy native stocks, while his father sneered and scolded because he would not go into the office.

Now he was left to himself with his plans and hopes. The dear mother was gone, but the hill was there--and Ella might come some day; there was a chance.

"What do you think of it?" he said to Patsy. Patsy was not Irish. He was an Italian from Tuscany; a farmer and forester by birth and breeding, a soldier by compulsion, an American citizen by choice.

"Fine!" said Patsy. "Fine. Ver' good. You do well."

They went over the ground together. "Could you build a little house here?" said Arnold. "Could you bring your wife? Could she attend to my house up there?--and could you keep hens and a cow and raise vegetables on this patch here--enough for all of us?--you to own the house and land--only you cannot sell it except to me?"

Then Patsy thanked his long neglected saints, imported his wife and little ones, took his eldest daughter out of the box factory, and his eldest son out of the printing office; and by the end of the summer they were comfortably established and ready to attend to the chestnut crop.

Arnold worked as hard as his man. Temporarily he hired other sturdy Italians, mechanics of experience; and spent his little store of capital in a way that would have made his father swear and his brother jeer at him.

When the year was over he had not much money left, but he had by his second waterfall a small electrical plant, with a printing office attached; and by the third a solid little mill, its turbine wheel running merrily in the ceaseless pour. Millstones cost more money than he thought, but there they were--brought up by night from the Hudson River--that his neighbors might not laugh too soon. Over the mill were large light rooms, pleasant to work in; with the shade of mighty trees upon the roof; and the sound of falling water in the sun.

By next summer this work was done, and the extra workmen gone. Whereat our poet refreshed himself with a visit to his

Ella, putting in some lazy weeks with her at Gloucester, happy and hopeful, but silent.

"How's the chestnut crop?" she asked him.

"Fine. Ver' good," he answered. "That's what Patsy says--and Patsy knows."

She pursued her inquiries. "Who cooks for you? Who keeps your camp in order? Who washes your clothes?"

"Mrs. Patsy," said he. "She's as good a cook as anybody need want."

"And how is the prospect?" asked Ella.

Arnold turned lazily over, where he lay on the sand at her feet, and looked at her long and hungrily. "The prospect," said he, "is divine."

Ella blushed and laughed and said he was a goose; but he kept on looking.

He wouldn't tell her much, though. "Don't, dear," he said when she urged for information. "It's too serious. If I should fail--"

"You won't fail!" she protested. "You can't fail! And if you do--why--as I told you before, I like to camp out!"

But when he tried to take some natural advantage of her friendliness she teased him--said he was growing to look just like his father! Which made them both laugh.

Arnold returned and settled down to business. He purchased stores of pasteboard, of paper, of printers ink, and a little machine to fold cartons. Thus equipped he retired to his fastness, and set dark-eyed Caterlina to work in a little box factory of his own; while clever Guiseppe ran the printing press, and Mafalda pasted. Cartons, piled flat, do not take up much room, even in thousands.

Then Arnold loafed deliberately.

"Why not your Mr. Blake work no more?" inquired Mrs. Patsy of her spouse.

"O he work--he work hard," replied Patsy. "You women--you not understand work!"

Mrs. Patsy tossed her head and answered in fluent Italian, so that her husband presently preferred out of doors occupation; but in truth Arnold Blake did not seem to do much that summer. He loafed under his great trees, regarding them lovingly; he loafed by his lonely upper waterfall, with happy dreaming eyes; he loafed in his little blue lake--floating face to the sky, care free and happy as a child. And if he scribbled a great deal--at any sudden moment when the fit seized him, why that was only his weakness as a poet.

Toward the end of September, he invited an old college friend up to see him; now a newspaper man--in the advertising department. These two seemed to have merry times together. They fished and walked and climbed, they talked much; and at night were heard roaring with laughter by their hickory fire.

"Have you got any money left?" demanded his friend.

"About a thou--" said Arnold. "And that's got to last me till next spring, you know."

"Blow it in--blow in every cent--it'll pay you. You can live through the winter somehow. How about transportation?"

"Got a nice electric dray--light and strong. Runs down hill with the load to tidewater, you see, and there's the old motorboat to take it down. Brings back supplies."

"Great!--It's simply great! Now, you save enough to eat till spring and give me the rest. Send me your stuff, all of it! and as soon as you get in a cent above expenses--send me that--I'll 'tend to the advertising!"

He did. He had only $800 to begin with. When the first profits began to come in he used them better; and as they rolled up he still spent them. Arnold began to feel anxious, to want to save money; but his friend replied: "You furnish the meal--I'll furnish the market!" And he did.

He began it in the subway in New York; that place of misery where eyes, ears, nose, and common self-respect are all offended, and even an advertisement is some relief.

"Hill" said the first hundred dollars, on a big blank space for a week. "Mill" said the second. "Hill Mill Meal," said the third.

The fourth was more explicit.

"When tired of every cereal
Try our new material--
 Hill Mill Meal."

The fifth--

"Ask your grocer if you feel
An interest in Hill Mill Meal.
 Samples free."

The sixth--
"A paradox! Surprising! True!
Made of chestnuts but brand new!
 Hill Mill Meal."

And the seventh--

"Solomon said it couldn't be done,
There wasn't a new thing under the sun--
 He never ate Hill Mill Meal!"

Seven hundred dollars went in this one method only; and
meanwhile diligent young men in automobiles were making
arrangements and leaving circulars and samples with the
grocer. Anybody will take free samples and everybody likes
chestnuts. Are they not the crown of luxury in turkey stuffing?
The gem of the confection as marron glaces? The sure profit of
the corner-merchant with his little charcoal stove, even when
they are half scorched and half cold? Do we not all love them,
roast, or boiled--only they are so messy to peel.

Arnold's only secret was his process; but his permanent advantage was in the fine quality of his nuts, and his exquisite care in manufacture. In dainty, neat, easily opened cartons (easily shut too, so they were not left gaping to gather dust), he put upon the market a sort of samp, chestnuts perfectly shelled and husked, roasted and ground, both coarse and fine. Good? You stood and ate half a package out of your hand, just tasting of it. Then you sat down and ate the other half.

He made pocket-size cartons, filled with whole ones, crafty man! And they became "The Business Man's Lunch" forthwith. A pocketful of roast chestnuts--and no mess nor trouble! And when they were boiled--well, we all know how good boiled chestnuts are. As to the meal, a new variety of mush appeared, and gems, muffins, and pancakes that made old epicures feel young again in the joys of a fresh taste, and gave America new standing in the eyes of France.

The orders rolled in and the poetry rolled out. The market for a new food is as wide as the world; and Jim Chamberlin was mad to conquer it, but Arnold explained to him that his total output was only so many bushels a year.

"Nonsense!" said Jim. "You're a--a--well, a poet! Come! Use your imagination! Look at these hills about you--they could grow chestnuts to the horizon! Look at this valley, that rattling river, a bunch of mills could run here! You can support a fine population--a whole village of people--there's no end to it, I tell you!"

"And where would my privacy be then and the beauty of the place?" asked Arnold, "I love this green island of chestnut trees, and the winding empty valley, just freckled with a few farms. I'd hate to support a village!"

"But you can be a Millionaire!" said Jim.

"I don't want to be a Millionaire," Arnold cheerfully replied.

Jim gazed at him, opening and shutting his mouth in silence. "You--confounded old--poet!" he burst forth at last.

"I can't help that," said Arnold.

"You'd better ask Miss Sutherland about it, I think," his friend drily suggested.

"To be sure! I had forgotten that--I will," the poet replied.

Then he invited her to come up and visit his Hill, met her at the train with the smooth, swift, noiseless, smell-less electric car, and held her hand in blissful silence as they rolled up the valley road. They wound more slowly up his graded avenue, green-arched by chestnut boughs.

He showed her the bit of meadowy inlet where the mill stood, by the heavy lower fall; the broad bright packing rooms above, where the busy Italian boys and girls chattered gaily as they worked. He showed her the second fall, with his little low-humming electric plant; a bluestone building, vine-covered, lovely, a tiny temple to the flower-god.

"It does our printing," said Arnold, "gives us light, heat and telephones. And runs the cars."

Then he showed her the shaded reaches of his lake, still, starred with lilies, lying dark under the curving boughs of water maples, doubling the sheer height of flower-crowned cliffs.

She held his hand tighter as they wound upward, circling the crown of the hill that she might see the splendid range of outlook; and swinging smoothly down a little and out on the green stretch before the house.

Ella gasped with delight. Gray, rough and harmonious, hung with woodbine and wildgrape, broad-porched and wide-windowed, it faced the setting sun. She stood looking, looking, over the green miles of tumbling hills, to the blue billowy far-off peaks swimming in soft light.

"There's the house," said Arnold, "furnished--there's a view room built on--for you, dear; I did it myself. There's the hill--and the little lake and one waterfall all for us! And the spring, and the garden, and some very nice Italians. And it will earn--my Hill and Mill, about three or four thousand dollars a year--above all expenses!"

"How perfectly splendid!" said Ella. "But there's one thing you've left out!"

"What's that?" he asked, a little dashed.

"You!" she answered. "Arnold Blake! My Poet!"

"Oh, I forgot," he added, after some long still moments. "I ought to ask you about this first. Jim Chamberlain says I can cover all these hills with chestnuts, fill this valley with people, string that little river with a row of mills, make breakfast for all the world--and be a Millionaire. Shall I?"

"For goodness sake--No!" said Ella. "Millionaire, indeed? And spoil the most perfect piece of living I ever saw or heard of!"

Then there was a period of bliss, indeed there was enough to last indefinitely.

But one pleasure they missed. They never saw even the astonished face, much less the highly irritated mind, of old John Blake, when he first returned from his two years of travel. The worst of it was he had eaten the stuff all the way home-and liked it! They told him it was Chestnut Meal--but that meant nothing to him. Then he began to find the jingling advertisements in every magazine; things that ran in his head and annoyed him.

> "When corn or rice no more are nice,
> When oatmeal seems to pall,
> When cream of wheat's no longer sweet
> And you abhor them all--"

"I do abhor them all!" the old man would vow, and take up a newspaper, only to read:

> "Better than any food that grows
> Upon or in the ground,
> Strong, pure and sweet
> And good to eat
> Our tree-born nuts are found."

"Bah!" said Mr. Blake, and tried another, which only
showed him:

"Good for mother, good for brother,
Good for child;
As for father--well, rather!
He's just wild."

He was. But the truth never dawned upon him till he
came to this one:

"About my hut
There grew a nut
Nutritious;
I could but feel
'Twould make a meal
Delicious.

I had a Hill,
I built a Mill
Upon it.
And hour by hour
I sought for power
To run it.

To burn my trees
Or try the breeze
Seemed crazy;
To use my arm
Had little charm--
I'm lazy!

The nuts are here,
But coal!--Quite dear
We find it!
We have the stuff.
Where's power enough
To grind it?

What force to find
My nuts to grind?
I've found it!
The Water-fall
Could beat 'em all--
And ground it!

PETER POETICUS."

"Confound your impudence!" he wrote to his son. "And
confound your poetic stupidity in not making a Big
Business now you've got a start! But I understand you
do make a living, and I'm thankful for that."

*

Arnold and Ella, watching the sunset from their
hammock, laughed softly together, and lived.

Charlotte Perkins Gilman

Three Thanksgivings

Andrew's letter and Jean's letter were in Mrs. Morrison's lap. She had read them both, and sat looking at them with a varying sort of smile, now motherly and now unmotherly.

"You belong with me," Andrew wrote. "It is not right that Jean's husband should support my mother. I can do it easily now. You shall have a good room and every comfort. The old house will let for enough to give you quite a little income of your own, or it can be sold and I will invest the money where you'll get a deal more out of it. It is not right that you should live alone there. Sally is old and liable to accident. I am anxious about you. Come on for Thanksgiving--and come to stay. Here is the money to come with. You know I want you. Annie joins me in sending love. ANDREW."

Mrs. Morrison read it all through again, and laid it down with her quiet, twinkling smile. Then she read Jean's.

"Now, mother, you've got to come to us for Thanksgiving this year. Just think! You haven't seen baby since he was three months old! And have never seen the twins. You won't know him--he's such a splendid big boy now. Joe says for you to come, of course. And, mother, why won't you come and live with us? Joe wants you, too. There's the little room upstairs; it's not very big, but we can put in a Franklin stove for you and make you pretty comfortable. Joe says he should think you ought to sell that white elephant of a place. He says he could put the money into his store and pay you good interest. I wish you would, mother. We'd just love to have you here. You'd be such a comfort to me, and such a help with the babies. And Joe just loves you. Do come now, and stay with us. Here is the money for the trip.--Your affectionate daughter, JEANNIE."

Mrs. Morrison laid this beside the other, folded both, and placed them in their respective envelopes, then in their several well-filled pigeon-holes in her big, old-fashioned desk. She turned and paced slowly up and down the long parlor, a tall woman, commanding of aspect, yet of a winningly attractive manner, erect and light-footed, still imposingly handsome.

It was now November, the last lingering boarder was long since gone, and a quiet winter lay before her. She was alone, but for Sally; and she smiled at Andrew's cautious expression, "liable to accident." He could not say "feeble" or "ailing," Sally being a colored lady of changeless aspect and incessant activity.

Mrs. Morrison was alone, and while living in the Welcome House she was never unhappy. Her father had built it, she was born there, she grew up playing on the broad green lawns in front, and in the acre of garden behind. It was the finest house in the village, and she then thought it the finest in the world.

Even after living with her father at Washington and abroad, after visiting hall, castle and palace, she still found the Welcome House beautiful and impressive.

If she kept on taking boarders she could live the year through, and pay interest, but not principal, on her little mortgage. This had been the one possible and necessary thing while the children were there, though it was a business she hated.

But her youthful experience in diplomatic circles, and the years of practical management in church affairs, enabled her to bear it with patience and success. The boarders often confided to one another, as they chatted and tatted on the long piazza, that Mrs. Morrison was "certainly very refined."

Now Sally whisked in cheerfully, announcing supper, and Mrs. Morrison went out to her great silver tea-tray at the lit end of the long, dark mahogany table, with as much dignity as if twenty titled guests were before her.

Afterward Mr. Butts called. He came early in the evening, with his usual air of determination and a somewhat unusual spruceness. Mr. Peter Butts was a florid, blonde person, a little stout, a little pompous, sturdy and immovable in the attitude of a self-made man. He had been a poor boy when she was a rich girl; and it gratified him much to realize--and to call upon her to realize--that their positions had changed. He meant no unkindness, his pride was honest and unveiled. Tact he had none.

She had refused Mr. Butts, almost with laughter, when he proposed to her in her gay girlhood. She had refused him, more gently, when he proposed to her in her early widowhood. He had always been her friend, and her husband's friend, a solid member of the church, and had taken the small mortgage of the house. She refused to allow him at first, but he was convincingly frank about it.

"This has nothing to do with my wanting you, Delia Morrison," he said. "I've always wanted you--and I've always wanted this house, too. You won't sell, but you've got to mortgage. By and by you can't pay up, and I'll get it--see? Then maybe you'll take me--to keep the house. Don't be a fool, Delia. It's a perfectly good investment."

She had taken the loan. She had paid the interest. She would pay the interest if she had to take boarders all her life. And she would not, at any price, marry Peter Butts.

He broached the subject again that evening, cheerful and undismayed. "You might as well come to it, Delia," he said. "Then we could live right here just the same. You aren't so young as you were, to be sure; I'm not, either. But you are as good a housekeeper as ever--better--you've had more experience."

"You are extremely kind, Mr. Butts," said the lady, "but I do not wish to marry you."

"I know you don't," he said. "You've made that clear. You don't, but I do. You've had your way and married the minister.

He was a good man, but he's dead. Now you might as well marry me."

"I do not wish to marry again, Mr. Butts; neither you nor anyone."

"Very proper, very proper, Delia," he replied. "It wouldn't look well if you did--at any rate, if you showed it. But why shouldn't you? The children are gone now--you can't hold them up against me any more."

"Yes, the children are both settled now, and doing nicely," she admitted.

"You don't want to go and live with them--either one of them-- do you?" he asked.

"I should prefer to stay here," she answered.

"Exactly! And you can't! You'd rather live here and be a grandee--but you can't do it. Keepin' house for boarders isn't any better than keepin' house for me, as I see. You'd much better marry me."

"I should prefer to keep the house without you, Mr. Butts."

"I know you would. But you can't, I tell you. I'd like to know what a woman of your age can do with a house like this--and no money? You can't live eternally on hens' eggs and garden truck. That won't pay the mortgage."

Mrs. Morrison looked at him with her cordial smile, calm and non-committal. "Perhaps I can manage it," she said.

"That mortgage falls due two years from Thanksgiving, you know."

"Yes--I have not forgotten."

"Well, then, you might just as well marry me now, and save two years of interest. It'll be my house, either way--but you'll be keepin' it just the same."

"It is very kind of you, Mr. Butts. I must decline the offer none the less. I can pay the interest, I am sure. And perhaps--in two years' time--I can pay the principal. It's not a large sum."

"That depends on how you look at it," said he. "Two thousand dollars is considerable money for a single woman to raise in two years--and interest."

He went away, as cheerful and determined as ever; and Mrs. Morrison saw him go with a keen, light in her fine eyes, a more definite line to that steady, pleasant smile.

Then she went to spend Thanksgiving with Andrew. He was glad to see her. Annie was glad to see her. They proudly installed her in "her room," and said she must call it "home" now.

This affectionately offered home was twelve by fifteen, and eight feet high. It had two windows, one looking at some pale gray clapboards within reach of a broom, the other giving a view of several small fenced yards occupied by cats, clothes and children. There was an ailanthus tree under the window, a lady ailanthus tree. Annie told her how profusely it bloomed. Mrs. Morrison particularly disliked the smell of ailanthus flowers. "It doesn't bloom in November," said she to herself. "I can be thankful for that!"

Andrew's church was very like the church of his father, and Mrs. Andrew was doing her best to fill the position of minister's wife--doing it well, too--there was no vacancy for a minister's mother.

Besides, the work she had done so cheerfully to help her husband was not what she most cared for, after all. She liked the people, she liked to manage, but she was not strong on doctrine. Even her husband had never known how far her views differed from his. Mrs. Morrison had never mentioned what they were.

Andrew's people were very polite to her. She was invited out with them, waited upon and watched over and set down among the old ladies and gentlemen--she had never realized so keenly that she was no longer young. Here nothing recalled her youth, every careful provision anticipated age. Annie brought her a hot-water bag at night, tucking it in at the foot of the bed with affectionate care. Mrs. Morrison thanked her, and subsequently took it out--airing the bed a little before she got into it. The house seemed very hot to her, after the big, windy halls at home.

The little dining-room, the little round table with the little round fern-dish in the middle, the little turkey and the little carving-set--game-set she would have called it--all made her feel as if she was looking through the wrong end of an opera-glass.

In Annie's precise efficiency she saw no room for her assistance; no room in the church, no room in the small, busy town, prosperous and progressive, and no room in the house. "Not enough to turn round in!" she said to herself. Annie, who had grown up in a city flat, thought their little parsonage palatial. Mrs. Morrison grew up in the Welcome House.

She stayed a week, pleasant and polite, conversational, interested in all that went on.

"I think your mother is just lovely," said Annie to Andrew.

"Charming woman, your mother," said the leading church member.

"What a delightful old lady your mother is!" said the pretty soprano.

And Andrew was deeply hurt and disappointed when she announced her determination to stay on for the present in her old home. "Dear boy," she said, "you mustn't take it to heart. I love to be with you, of course, but I love my home, and want to keep it is long as I can. It is a great pleasure to see you and Annie so well settled, and so happy together. I am most truly thankful for you."

"My home is open to you whenever you wish to come, mother," said Andrew. But he was a little angry.

Mrs. Morrison came home as eager as a girl, and opened her own door with her own key, in spite of Sally's haste.

Two years were before her in which she must find some way to keep herself and Sally, and to pay two thousand dollars and the interest to Peter Butts. She considered her assets. There was the house--the white elephant. It was big--very big. It was profusely furnished. Her father had entertained lavishly like the Southern-born, hospitable gentleman he was; and the bedrooms ran in suites--somewhat deteriorated by the use of boarders, but still numerous and habitable. Boarders--she abhorred them. They were people from afar, strangers and interlopers. She went over the place from garret to cellar, from front gate to backyard fence.

The garden had great possibilities. She was fond of gardening. and understood it well. She measured and estimated.

"This garden," she finally decided, "with the hens, will feed us two women and sell enough to pay Sally. If we make plenty of jelly, it may cover the coal bill, too. As to clothes--I don't need any. They last admirably. I can manage. I can live--but two thousand dollars--and interest!"

In the great attic was more furniture, discarded sets put there when her extravagant young mother had ordered new ones. And chairs--uncounted chairs. Senator Welcome used to invite numbers to meet his political friends--and they had delivered glowing orations in the wide, double parlors, the impassioned speakers standing on a temporary dais, now in the cellar; and the enthusiastic listeners disposed more or less comfortably on these serried rows of "folding chairs," which folded sometimes, and let down the visitor in scarlet confusion to the floor.

She sighed as she remembered those vivid days and glittering nights. She used to steal downstairs in her little pink wrapper and listen to the eloquence. It delighted her young soul to see her father rising on his toes, coming down sharply on his heels, hammering one hand upon the other; and then to hear the fusilade of applause.

Here were the chairs, often borrowed for weddings, funerals, and church affairs, somewhat worn and depleted, but still numerous. She mused upon them. Chairs--hundreds of chairs. They would sell for very little.

She went through her linen room. A splendid stock in the old days; always carefully washed by Sally; surviving even the boarders. Plenty of bedding, plenty of towels, plenty of napkins and tablecloths. "It would make a good hotel--but I can't have it so--I can't! Besides, there's no need of another hotel here. The poor little Haskins House is never full."

The stock in the china closet was more damaged than some other things, naturally; but she inventoried it with care. The countless cups of crowded church receptions were especially prominent. Later additions these, not very costly cups, but numerous, appallingly.

When she had her long list of assets all in order, she sat and studied it with a clear and daring mind. Hotel--boarding-house--she could think of nothing else. School! A girls' school! A boarding school! There was money to be made at that, and fine work done. It was a brilliant thought at first, and she gave several hours, and much paper and ink, to its full consideration. But she would need some capital for advertising; she must engage teachers--adding to her definite obligation; and to establish it, well, it would require time.

Mr. Butts, obstinate, pertinacious, oppressively affectionate, would give her no time. He meant to force her to marry him for her own good--and his. She shrugged her fine shoulders with a little shiver. Marry Peter Butts! Never! Mrs. Morrison still loved her husband. Some day she meant to see him again--God willing--and she did not wish to have to tell him that at fifty she had been driven into marrying Peter Butts.

Better live with Andrew. Yet when she thought of living with Andrew, she shivered again. Pushing back her sheets of figures and lists of personal property, she rose to her full graceful height and began to walk the floor. There was plenty of floor to walk. She considered, with a set deep thoughtfulness, the town and the townspeople, the surrounding country, the hundreds upon hundreds of women whom she knew--and liked, and who liked her.

It used to be said of Senator Welcome that he had no enemies; and some people, strangers, maliciously disposed, thought it no credit to his character. His daughter had no enemies, but no one had ever blamed her for her unlimited friendliness. In her father's wholesale entertainments the whole town knew and admired his daughter; in her husband's popular church she had come to know the women of the countryside about them. Her mind strayed off to these women, farmers' wives, comfortably off in a plain way, but starving for companionship, for occasional stimulus and pleasure. It was one of her joys in her husband's time to bring together these women--to teach and entertain them.

Suddenly she stopped short in the middle of the great high-ceiled room, and drew her head up proudly like a victorious queen. One wide, triumphant, sweeping glance she cast at the well-loved walls--and went back to her desk, working swiftly, excitedly, well into the hours of the night.

*

Presently the little town began to buzz, and the murmur ran far out into the surrounding country. Sunbonnets wagged over fences; butcher carts and pedlar's wagon carried the news farther; and ladies visiting found one topic in a thousand houses.

Mrs. Morrison was going to entertain. Mrs. Morrison had invited the whole feminine population, it would appear, to meet Mrs. Isabelle Carter Blake, of Chicago. Even Haddleton had heard of Mrs. Isabelle Carter Blake. And even Haddleton had nothing but admiration for her.

She was known the world over for her splendid work for children--for the school children and the working children of the country. Yet she was known also to have lovingly and wisely reared six children of her own--and made her husband happy in his home. On top of that she had lately written a novel, a popular novel, of which everyone was talking; and on top of that she was an intimate friend of a certain conspicuous Countess--an Italian.

It was even rumored, by some who knew Mrs. Morrison better than others--or thought they did--that the Countess was coming, too! No one had known before that Delia Welcome was a school-mate of Isabel Carter, and a lifelong friend; and that was ground for talk in itself.

The day arrived, and the guests arrived. They came in hundreds upon hundreds, and found ample room in the great white house.

The highest dream of the guests was realized--the Countess had come, too. With excited joy they met her, receiving impressions that would last them for all their lives, for those large widening waves of reminiscence which delight us the more as years pass. It was an incredible glory--Mrs. Isabelle Carter Blake, and a Countess!

Some were moved to note that Mrs. Morrison looked the easy peer of these eminent ladies, and treated the foreign nobility precisely as she did her other friends.

She spoke, her clear quiet voice reaching across the murmuring din, and silencing it.

"Shall we go into the east room? If you will all take chairs in the east room, Mrs. Blake is going to be so kind as to address us. Also perhaps her friend--"

They crowded in, sitting somewhat timorously on the unfolded chairs.

Then the great Mrs. Blake made them an address of memorable power and beauty, which received vivid sanction from that imposing presence in Parisian garments on the platform by her side. Mrs. Blake spoke to them of the work she was interested in, and how it was aided everywhere by the women's clubs. She gave them the number of these clubs, and described with contagious enthusiasm the inspiration of their great meetings. She spoke of the women's club houses, going up in city after city, where many associations meet and help one another. She was winning and convincing and most entertaining--an extremely attractive speaker.

Had they a women's club there? They had not.

Not yet, she suggested, adding that it took no time at all to make one.

They were delighted and impressed with Mrs. Blake's speech, but its effect was greatly intensified by the address of the Countess.

"I, too, am American," she told them; "born here, reared in England, married in Italy." And she stirred their hearts with a vivid account of the women's clubs and associations all over Europe, and what they were accomplishing. She was going back soon, she said, the wiser and happier for this visit to her native land, and she should remember particularly this beautiful, quiet town, trusting that if she came to it again it would have joined the great sisterhood of women, "whose hands were touching around the world for the common good."

It was a great occasion.

The Countess left next day, but Mrs. Blake remained, and spoke in some of the church meetings, to an ever widening circle of admirers. Her suggestions were practical.

"What you need here is a 'Rest and Improvement Club,'" she said. "Here are all you women coming in from the country to do your shopping--and no place to go to. No place to lie down if you're tired, to meet a friend, to eat your lunch in peace, to do your hair. All you have to do is organize, pay some small regular due, and provide yourselves with what you want."

There was a volume of questions and suggestions, a little opposition, much random activity.

Who was to do it? Where was there a suitable place? They would have to hire someone to take charge of it. It would only be used once a week. It would cost too much.

Mrs. Blake, still practical, made another suggestion. Why not combine business with pleasure, and make use of the best place in town, if you can get it? I think Mrs. Morrison could be persuaded to let you use part of her house; it's quite too big for one woman."

Then Mrs. Morrison, simple and cordial as ever, greeted with warm enthusiasm by her wide circle of friends.

"I have been thinking this over," she said. "Mrs. Blake has been discussing it with me. My house is certainly big enough for all of you, and there am I, with nothing to do but entertain you. Suppose you formed such a club as you speak of--for Rest and

Improvement. My parlors are big enough for all manner of meetings; there are bedrooms in plenty for resting. If you form such a club I shall be glad to help with my great, cumbersome house, shall be delighted to see so many friends there so often; and I think I could furnish accommodations more cheaply than you could manage in any other way.

Then Mrs. Blake gave them facts and figures, showing how much clubhouses cost--and how little this arrangement would cost. "Most women have very little money, I know," she said, "and they hate to spend it on themselves when they have; but even a little money from each goes a long way when it is put together. I fancy there are none of us so poor we could not squeeze out, say ten cents a week. For a hundred women that would be ten dollars. Could you feed a hundred tired women for ten dollars, Mrs. Morrison?"

Mrs. Morrison smiled cordially. "Not on chicken pie," she said, "But I could give them tea and coffee, crackers and cheese for that, I think. And a quiet place to rest, and a reading room, and a place to hold meetings."

Then Mrs. Blake quite swept them off their feet by her wit and eloquence. She gave them to understand that if a share in the palatial accommodation of the Welcome House, and as good tea and coffee as old Sally made, with a place to meet, a place to rest, a place to talk, a place to lie down, could be had for ten cents a week each, she advised them to clinch the arrangement at once before Mrs. Morrison's natural good sense had overcome her enthusiasm.

Before Mrs. Isabelle Carter Blake had left, Haddleton had a large and eager women's club, whose entire expenses, outside of stationary and postage, consisted of ten cents a week per capita, paid to Mrs. Morrison. Everybody belonged. It was open at once for charter members, and all pressed forward to claim that privileged place.

They joined by hundreds, and from each member came this tiny sum to Mrs. Morrison each week. It was very little money, taken separately. But it added up with silent speed. Tea and coffee, purchased in bulk, crackers by the barrel, and whole cheeses--these are not expensive luxuries. The town was full of Mrs. Morrison's ex-Sunday-school boys, who furnished her with the best they had--at cost. There was a good deal of work, a good deal of care, and room for the whole supply of Mrs. Morrison's diplomatic talent and experience. Saturdays found the Welcome House as full as it could hold, and Sundays found Mrs. Morrison in bed. But she liked it.

A busy, hopeful year flew by, and then she went to Jean's for Thanksgiving.

The room Jean gave her was about the same size as her haven in Andrew's home, but one flight higher up, and with a sloping ceiling. Mrs. Morrison whitened her dark hair upon it, and rubbed her head confusedly. Then she shook it with renewed determination.

The house was full of babies. There was little Joe, able to get about, and into everything. There were the twins, and there was the new baby. There was one servant, over-worked and cross. There was a small, cheap, totally inadequate nursemaid. There

95

was Jean, happy but tired, full of joy, anxiety and affection, proud of her children, proud of her husband, and delighted to unfold her heart to her mother.

By the hour she babbled of their cares and hopes, while Mrs. Morrison, tall and elegant in her well-kept old black silk, sat holding the baby or trying to hold the twins. The old silk was pretty well finished by the week's end. Joseph talked to her also, telling her how well he was getting on, and how much he needed capital, urging her to come and stay with them; it was such a help to Jeannie; asking questions about the house.

There was no going visiting here. Jeannie could not leave the babies. And few visitors; all the little suburb being full of similarly overburdened mothers. Such as called found Mrs. Morrison charming. What she found them, she did not say. She bade her daughter an affectionate good-bye when the week was up, smiling at their mutual contentment.

"Good-bye, my dear children," she said. "I am so glad for all your happiness. I am thankful for both of you."

But she was more thankful to get home.

Mr. Butts did not have to call for his interest this time, but he called none the less.

"How on earth'd you get it, Delia?" he demanded. "Screwed it out o' these club-women?"

"Your interest is so moderate, Mr. Butts, that it is easier to meet than you imagine," was her answer. "Do you know the average interest they charge in Colorado? The women vote there, you know."

He went away with no more personal information than that; and no nearer approach to the twin goals of his desire than the passing of the year.

"One more year, Delia," he said; "then you'll have to give in."

"One more year!" she said to herself, and took up her chosen task with renewed energy.

The financial basis of the undertaking was very simple, but it would never have worked so well under less skilful management. Five dollars a year these country women could not have faced, but ten cents a week was possible to the poorest. There was no difficulty in collecting, for they brought it themselves; no unpleasantness in receiving, for old Sally stood at the receipt of custom and presented the covered cash box when they came for their tea.

On the crowded Saturdays the great urns were set going, the mighty array of cups arranged in easy reach, the ladies filed by, each taking her refection and leaving her dime. Where the effort came was in enlarging the membership and keeping up the attendance, and this effort was precisely in the line of Mrs. Morrison's splendid talents.

Serene, cheerful, inconspicuously active, planning like the born statesman she was, executing like a practical politician, Mrs. Morrison gave her mind to the work, and thrived upon it. Circle within circle, and group within group, she set small classes and departments at work, having a boys' club by and by in the big room over the woodshed, girls' clubs, reading clubs, study clubs, little meetings of every sort that were not held in churches, and some that were--previously.

For each and all there was, if wanted, tea and coffee, crackers and cheese; simple fare, of unvarying excellence, and from each and all, into the little cashbox, ten cents for these refreshments. From the club members this came weekly; and the club members, kept up by a constant variety of interests, came every week. As to numbers, before the first six months was over The Haddleton Rest and Improvement Club numbered five hundred women.

Now, five hundred times ten cents a week is twenty-six hundred dollars a year. Twenty-six hundred dollars a year would not be very much to build or rent a large house, to furnish five hundred people with chairs, lounges, books, and magazines, dishes and service; and with food and drink even of the simplest. But if you are miraculously supplied with a club-house, furnished, with a manager and servant on the spot, then that amount of money goes a long way.

On Saturdays Mrs. Morrison hired two helpers for half a day, for half a dollar each. She stocked the library with many magazines for fifty dollars a year. She covered fuel, light, and small miscellanies with another hundred. And she fed her multitude with the plain viands agreed upon, at about four cents apiece.

For her collateral entertainments, her many visits, the various new expenses entailed, she paid as well; and yet at the end of the first year she had not only her interest, but a solid thousand dollars of clear profit. With a calm smile she surveyed it, heaped in neat stacks of bills in the small safe in the wall behind her bed. Even Sally did not know it was there.

The second season was better than the first. There were difficulties, excitements, even some opposition, but she rounded out the year triumphantly. "After that," she said to herself, "they may have the deluge if they like."

She made all expenses, made her interest, made a little extra cash, clearly her own, all over and above the second thousand dollars.

Then did she write to son and daughter, inviting them and their families to come home to Thanksgiving, and closing each letter with joyous pride: "Here is the money to come with."

They all came, with all the children and two nurses. There was plenty of room in the Welcome House, and plenty of food on the long mahogany table. Sally was as brisk as a bee, brilliant in scarlet and purple; Mrs. Morrison carved her big turkey with queenly grace.

"I don't see that you're over-run with club women, mother," said Jeannie.

"It's Thanksgiving, you know; they're all at home. I hope they are all as happy, as thankful for their homes as I am for mine," said Mrs. Morrison.

Afterward Mr. Butts called. With dignity and calm unruffled, Mrs. Morrison handed him his interest--and principal.

Mr. Butts was almost loath to receive it, though his hand automatically grasped the crisp blue check.

"I didn't know you had a bank account," he protested, somewhat dubiously.

"Oh, yes; you'll find the check will be honored, Mr. Butts."

"I'd like to know how you got this money. You can't 'a' skinned it out o' that club of yours."

"I appreciate your friendly interest, Mr. Butts; you have been most kind."

"I believe some of these great friends of yours have lent it to you. You won't be any better off, I can tell you."

"Come, come, Mr. Butts! Don't quarrel with good money. Let us part friends."

And they parted.

When I Was a Witch

If I had understood the terms of that one-sided contract with Satan, the Time of Witching would have lasted longer--you may be sure of that. But how was I to tell? It just happened, and has never happened again, though I've tried the same preliminaries as far as I could control them.

The thing began all of a sudden, one October midnight--the 30th, to be exact. It had been hot, really hot, all day, and was sultry and thunderous in the evening; no air stirring, and the whole house stewing with that ill-advised activity which always seems to move the steam radiator when it isn't wanted.

I was in a state of simmering rage--hot enough, even without the weather and the furnace--and I went up on the roof to cool off. A top-floor apartment has that advantage, among others-- you can take a walk without the mediation of an elevator boy!

There are things enough in New York to lose one's temper over at the best of times, and on this particular day they seemed to all happen at once, and some fresh ones. The night before, cats and dogs had broken my rest, of course. My morning paper was more than usually mendacious; and my neighbor's morning paper--more visible than my own as I went down town--was more than usually salacious. My cream wasn't cream--my egg was a relic of the past. My "new" napkins were giving out.

Being a woman, I'm supposed not to swear; but when the motorman disregarded my plain signal, and grinned as he rushed by; when the subway guard waited till I was just about to step on board and then slammed the door in my face-- standing behind it calmly for some minutes before the bell rang to warrant his closing--I desired to swear like a mule-driver.

At night it was worse. The way people paw one's back in the crowd! The cow-puncher who packs the people in or jerks them out--the men who smoke and spit, law or no law--the women whose saw-edged cart-wheel hats, swashing feathers and deadly pins, add so to one's comfort inside.

Well, as I said, I was in a particularly bad temper, and went up on the roof to cool off. Heavy black clouds hung low overhead, and lightning flickered threateningly here and there.

A starved, black cat stole from behind a chimney and mewed dolefully. Poor thing! She had been scalded.

The street was quiet for New York. I leaned over a little and looked up and down the long parallels of twinkling lights. A belated cab drew near, the horse so tired he could hardly hold his head up.

Then the driver, with a skill born of plenteous practice, flung out his long-lashed whip and curled it under the poor beast's belly with a stinging cut that made me shudder. The horse shuddered too, poor wretch, and jingled his harness with an effort at a trot.

I leaned over the parapet and watched that man with a spirit of unmitigated ill-will.

"I wish," said I, slowly--and I did wish it with all my heart--"that every person who strikes or otherwise hurts a horse unnecessarily, shall feel the pain intended--and the horse not feel it!"

It did me good to say it, anyhow, but I never expected any result. I saw the man swing his great whip again, and--lay on heartily. I saw him throw up his hands--heard him scream--but I never thought what the matter was, even then.

The lean, black cat, timid but trustful, rubbed against my skirt and mewed.

"Poor Kitty" I said; "poor Kitty! It is a shame!" And I thought tenderly of all the thousands of hungry, hunted cats who stink and suffer its a great city.

Later, when I tried to sleep, and up across the stillness rose the raucous shrieks of some of these same sufferers, my pity turned cold. "Any fool that will try to keep a cat in a city!" I muttered, angrily.

Another yell--a pause--an ear-torturing, continuous cry. "I wish," I burst forth, "that every cat in the city was comfortably dead!"

A sudden silence fell, and in course of time I got to sleep.

Things went fairly well next morning, till I tried another egg. They were expensive eggs, too.

"I can't help it!" said my sister, who keeps house.

"I know you can't," I admitted. "But somebody could help it. I wish the people who are responsible had to eat their old eggs, and never get a good one till they sold good ones!"

"They'd stop eating eggs, that's all," said my sister, "and eat meat."

"Let 'em eat meat!" I said, recklessly. "The meat is as bad as the eggs! It's so long since we've had a clean, fresh chicken that I've forgotten how they taste!"

"It's cold storage," said my sister. She is a peaceable sort; I'm not.

"Yes, cold storage!" I snapped. "It ought to be a blessing--to tide over shortages, equalize supplies, and lower prices. What does it do? Corner the market, raise prices the year round, and make all the food bad!"

My anger rose. "If there was any way of getting at them!" I cried. "The law don't touch 'em. They need to be cursed

104

somehow! I'd like to do it! I wish the whole crowd that profit by this vicious business might taste their bad meat, their old fish, their stale milk--whatever they ate. Yes, and feel the prices as we do!"

"They couldn't you know; they're rich," said my sister.

"I know that," I admitted, sulkily. "There's no way of getting at 'em. But I wish they could. And I wish they knew how people hated 'em, and felt that, too--till they mended their ways!"

When I left for my office I saw a funny thing. A man who drove a garbage cart took his horse by the bits and jerked and wrenched brutally. I was amazed to see him clap his hands to his own jaws with a moan, while the horse philosophically licked his chops and looked at him.

The man seemed to resent his expression, and struck him on the head, only to rub his own poll and swear amazedly, looking around to see who had hit him. the horse advanced a step, stretching a hungry nose toward a garbage pail crowned with cabbage leaves, and the man, recovering his sense of proprietorship, swore at him and kicked him in the ribs. That time he had to sit down, turning pale and weak. I watched with growing wonder and delight.

A market wagon came clattering down the street; the hard-faced young ruffian fresh for his morning task. He gathered the ends of the reins and brought them down on the horse's back with a resounding thwack. The horse did not notice this at all, but the boy did. He yelled!

I came to a place where many teamsters were at work hauling dirt and crushed stone. A strange silence and peace hung over the scene where usually the sound of the lash and sight of brutal blows made me hurry by. The men were talking together a little, and seemed to be exchanging notes. It was too good to be true. I gazed and marvelled, waiting for my car.

It came, merrily running along. It was not full. There was one not far ahead, which I had missed in watching the horses; there was no other near it in the rear.

Yet the coarse-faced person in authority who ran it, went gaily by without stopping, though I stood on the track almost, and waved my umbrella.

A hot flush of rage surged to my face. "I wish you felt the blow you deserve," said I, viciously, looking after the car. "I wish you'd have to stop, and back to here, and open the door and apologize. I wish that would happen to all of you, every time you play that trick."

To my infinite amazement, that car stopped and backed till the front door was before me. The motorman opened it. holding his hand to his cheek. "Beg your pardon, madam!" he said.

I passed in, dazed, overwhelmed. Could it be? Could it possibly be that--that what I wished came true. The idea sobered me, but I dismissed it with a scornful smile. "No such luck!" said I.

Opposite me sat a person in petticoats. She was of a sort I particularly detest. No real body of bones and muscles, but the contours of grouped sausages. Complacent, gaudily dressed, heavily wigged and ratted, with powder and perfume and flowers and jewels--and a dog.

A poor, wretched, little, artificial dog--alive, but only so by virtue of man's insolence; not a real creature that God made. And the dog had clothes on--and a bracelet! His fitted jacket had a pocket--and a pocket-handkerchief! He looked sick and unhappy.

I meditated on his pitiful position, and that of all the other poor chained prisoners, leading unnatural lives of enforced celibacy, cut off from sunlight, fresh air, the use of their limbs; led forth at stated intervals by unwilling servants, to defile our streets; over-fed, under-exercised, nervous and unhealthy.

"And we say we love them!" said I, bitterly to myself. "No wonder they bark and howl and go mad. No wonder they have almost as many diseases as we do! I wish--" Here the thought I had dismissed struck me agin. "I wish that all the unhappy dogs in cities would die at once!"

I watched the sad-eyed little invalid across the car. He dropped his head and died. She never noticed it till she got off; then she made fuss enough.

The evening papers were full of it. Some sudden pestilence had struck both dogs and cats, it would appear. Red headlines struck the eye, big letters, and columns were filled out of the complaints of those who had lost their "pets," of the sudden labors of the board of health, and interviews with doctors.

All day, as I went through the office routine, the strange sense of this new power struggled with reason and common knowledge. I even tried a few furtive test "wishes"--wished that the waste basket would fall over, that the inkstand would fill itself; but they didn't.

I dismissed the idea as pure foolishness, till I saw those newspapers, and heard people telling worse stories.

One thing I decided at once--not to tell a soul. "Nobody'd believe me if I did," said I to myself. "And I won't give 'em the chance. I've scored on cats and dogs, anyhow--and horses."

As I watched the horses at work that afternoon, and thought of all their unknown sufferings from crowded city stables, bad air and insufficient food, and from the wearing strain of asphalt pavements in wet and icy weather, I decided to have another try on horses.

"I wish," said I, slowly and carefully, but with a fixed intensity of purposes, "that every horse owner, keeper, hirer and driver or rider, might feel what the horse feels, when he suffers at our hands. Feel it keenly and constantly till the case is mended."

I wasn't able to verify this attempt for some time; but the effect was so general that it got widely talked about soon; and this "new wave of humane feeling" soon raised the status of horses in our city. Also it diminished their numbers. People began to prefer motor drays--which was a mighty good thing.

Now I felt pretty well assured in my own mind, and kept my assurance to my self. Also I began to make a list of my cherished grudges, with a fine sense of power and pleasure.

"I must be careful," I said to myself; "very careful; and, above all things, make the punishment fit the crime."

The subway crowding came to my mind next; both the people who crowd because they have to, and the people who make them. "I mustn't punish anybody, for what they can't help," I mused. "But when it's pure meanness!" Then I bethought me of the remote stockholders, of the more immediate directors, of the painfully prominent officials and insolent employees--and got to work.

"I might as well make a good job of it while this lasts," said I to myself. "It's quite a responsibility, but lots of fun." And I wished that every person responsible for the condition of our subways might be mysteriously compelled to ride up and down in them continuously during rush hours.

This experiment I watched with keen interest, but for the life of me I could see little difference. There were a few more well-dressed persons in the crowds, that was all. So I came to the conclusion that the general public was mostly to blame, and carried their daily punishment without knowing it.

For the insolent guards and cheating ticket-sellers who give you short change, very slowly, when you are dancing on one foot and your train is there, I merely wished that they might feel the pain their victims would like to give them, short of real injury. They did, I guess.

Then I wished similar things for all manner of corporations and officials. It worked. It worked amazingly. There was a sudden conscientious revival all over the country. The dry bones rattled and sat up. Boards of directors, having troubles enough of their own, were aggravated by innumerable communications from suddenly sensitive stockholders.

In mills and mints and railroads, things began to mend. The country buzzed. The papers fattened. The churches sat up and took credit to themselves. I was incensed at this; and, after brief consideration, wished that every minister would preach to his congregation exactly what he believed and what he thought of them.

I went to six services the next Sunday--about ten minutes each, for two sessions. It was most amusing. A thousand pulpits were emptied forthwith, refilled, re-emptied, and so on, from week to week. People began to go to church; men largely--women didn't like it as well. They had always supposed the ministers thought more highly of them than now appeared to be the case.

One of my oldest grudges was against the sleeping-car people; and now I began to consider them. How often I had grinned and borne it--with other thousands--submitting helplessly.

Here is a railroad--a common carrier--and you have to use it. You pay for your transportation, a good round sum.

Then if you wish to stay in the sleeping car during the day, they charge you another two dollars and a half for the privilege of sitting there, whereas you have paid for a seat when you bought your ticket. That seat is now sold to another person--twice sold! Five dollars for twenty-four hours in a space six feet by three by three at night, and one seat by day; twenty-four of these privileges to a car--$120 a day for the rent of the car--and the passengers to pay the porter besides. That makes $44,800 a year.

Sleeping cars are expensive to build, they say. So are hotels; but they do not charge at such a rate. Now, what could I do to get even? Nothing could ever put back the dollars into the millions of pockets; but it might be stopped now, this beautiful process.

So I wished that all persons who profited by this performance might feel a shame so keen that they would make public avowal and apology, and, as partial restitution, offer their wealth to promote the cause of free railroads!

Then I remembered parrots. This was lucky, for my wrath flamed again. It was really cooling, as I tried to work out responsibility and adjust penalties. But parrots! Any person who wants to keep a parrot should go and live on an island alone with their preferred conversationalist!

There was a huge, squawky parrot right across the street from me, adding its senseless, rasping cries to the more necessary evils of other noises.

I had also an aunt with a parrot. She was a wealthy, ostentatious person, who had been an only child and inherited her money.

Uncle Joseph hated the yelling bird, but that didn't make any difference to Aunt Mathilda.

I didn't like this aunt, and wouldn't visit her, lest she think I was truckling for the sake of her money; but after I had wished this time, I called at the time set for my curse to work; and it did work with a vengeance. There sat poor Uncle Joe, looking thinner and meeker than ever; and my aunt, like an overripe plum, complacent enough.

"Let me out!" said Polly, suddenly. "Let me out to take a walk!"

"The clever thing!" said Aunt Mathilda. "He never said that before."

She let him out. Then he flapped up on the chandelier and sat among the prisms, quite safe.

"What an old pig you are, Mathilda!" said the parrot.

She started to her feet--naturally.

"Born a Pig--trained a Pig--a Pig by nature and education!" said the parrot. "Nobody'd put up with you, except for your money; unless it's this long-suffering husband of yours. He wouldn't, if he hadn't the patience of Job!"

"Hold your tongue!" screamed Aunt Mathilda. "Come down from there! Come here!"

Polly cocked his head and jingled the prisms. "Sit down, Mathilda!" he said, cheerfully. "You've got to listen. You are fat and homely and selfish. You are a nuisance to everybody about you. You have got to feed me and take care of me better than ever--and you've got to listen to me when I talk. Pig!"

I visited another person with a parrot the next day. She put a cloth over his cage when I came in.

"Take it off!" said Polly. She took it off.

"Won't you come into the other room?" she asked me, nervously.

"Better stay here!" said her pet. "Sit still--sit still!"

She sat still.

"Your hair is mostly false," said pretty Poll. "And your teeth--and your outlines. You eat too much. You are lazy. You ought to exercise, and don't know enough. Better apologize to this lady for backbiting! You've got to listen."

The trade in parrots fell off from that day; they say there is no call for them. But the people who kept parrots, keep them yet--parrots live a long time.

Bores were a class of offenders against whom I had long borne undying enmity. Now I rubbed my hands and began on them, with this simple wish: That every person whom they bored should tell them the plain truth.

There is one man whom I have specially in mind. He was blackballed at a pleasant club, but continues to go there. He isn't a member--he just goes; and no one does anything to him.

It was very funny after this. He appeared that very night at a meeting, and almost every person present asked him how he came there. "You're not a member, you know," they said. "Why do you butt in? Nobody likes you."

Some were more lenient with him. "Why don't you learn to be more considerate of others, and make some real friends?" they said. "To have a few friends who do enjoy your visits ought to be pleasanter than being a public nuisance."

He disappeared from that club, anyway.

I began to feel very cocky indeed.

In the food business there was already a marked improvement; and in transportation. The hubbub of reformation waxed louder daily, urged on by the unknown sufferings of all the profiters by iniquity.

The papers thrived on all this; and as I watched the loud-voiced protestations of my pet abomination in journalism, I had a brilliant idea, literally.

Next morning I was down town early, watching the men open their papers. My abomination was shamefully popular, and never more so than this morning. Across the top was printing in gold letters:

All intentional lies, in adv., editorial, news, or any other
column. . .Scarlet
All malicious matter. . .Crimson
All careless or ignorant mistakes. . .Pink
All for direct self-interest of owner. . .Dark green
All mere bait--to sell the paper. . .Bright green
All advertising, primary or secondary. . .Brown
All sensational and salacious matter. . .Yellow
All hired hypocrisy. . .Purple
Good fun, instruction and entertainment. . .Blue
True and necessary news and honest editorials. . .Ordinary
print

You never saw such a crazy quilt of a paper. They were bought
like hot cakes for some days; but the real business fell off very
soon. They'd have stopped it all if they could; but the papers
looked all right when they came off the press. The color
scheme flamed out only to the bona-fide reader.

I let this work for about a week, to the immense joy of all the
other papers; and then turned it on to them, all at once.
Newspaper reading became very exciting for a little, but the
trade fell off. Even newspaper editors could not keep on
feeding a market like that. The blue printed and ordinary
printed matter grew from column to column and page to page.
Some papers--small, to be sure, but refreshing--began to appear
in blue and black alone.

This kept me interested and happy for quite a while; so much
so that I quite forgot to be angry at other things. There was
such a change in all kinds of business, following the mere
printing of truth in the newspapers. It began to appear as if we

had lived in a sort of delirium--not really knowing the facts
about anything. As soon as we really knew the facts, we began
to behave very differently, of course.

What really brought all my enjoyment to an end was women.
Being a woman, I was naturally interested in them, and could
see some things more clearly than men could. I saw their real
power, their real dignity, their real responsibility in the world;
and then the way they dress and behave used to make me fairly
frantic. 'Twas like seeing archangels playing jackstraws--or
real horses only used as rocking-horses. So I determined to get
after them.

How to manage it! What to hit first! Their hats, their ugly,
inane, outrageous hats--that is what one thinks of first. Their
silly, expensive clothes--their diddling beads and jewelry--their
greedy childishness--mostly of the women provided for by rich
men.

Then I thought of all the other women, the real ones, the vast
majority, patiently doing the work of servants without even a
servant's pay--and neglecting the noblest duties of motherhood
in favor of house-service; the greatest power on earth, blind,
chained, untaught, in a treadmill. I thought of what they might
do, compared to what they did do, and my heart swelled with
something that was far from anger.

Then I wished--with all my strength--that women, all women,
might realize Womanhood at last; its power and pride and
place in life; that they might see their duty as mothers of the
world--to love and care for everyone alive; that they might see
their dirty to men--to choose only the best, and then to bear and

rear better ones; that they might see their duty as human beings, and come right out into full life and work and happiness!

I stopped, breathless, with shining eyes. I waited, trembling, for things to happen.

Nothing happened.

You see, this magic which had fallen on me was black magic-- and I had wished white.

It didn't work at all, and, what was worse, it stopped all the other things that were working so nicely.

Oh, if I had only thought to wish permanence for those lovely punishments! If only I had done more while I could do it, had half appreciated my privileges when I was a Witch!

Charlotte Perkins Gilman

My Astonishing Dodo

She was twenty-six, and owned it cheerfully, the day I met her.

This prejudiced me in her favor at once, for I prize honesty in women, and on this point it is unusual. She did not, it is true, share largely in my special artistic tastes, or, to any great extent, in my social circle; but she was a fine wholesome sweet woman, cheerful and strong, and I wished to make a friend of her. I greatly prized my good friends among women, for I had conscientious views against marrying on a small salary.

Later it appeared that she had other and different views, but she did not mention them then.

Dorothea was her name. Her family called her Dora, her intimate friends, Dolly, but I called her Dodo, just between ourselves.

A very good-looking girl was Dodo, though not showy; and in no way distinguished in dress, which rather annoyed me at

119

first; for I have a great admiration for a well-gowned, well-groomed woman.

My ideas on matrimony were strongly colored by certain facts and figures given me by an old college friend of mine. He was a nice fellow, and his wife one of the loveliest girls of our set, though rather delicate. They lived very comfortably in a quiet way, with a few good books and pictures, and four little ones.

"It's a thousand dollars a year for the first year for each baby," he told me, "and five hundred a year afterward."

I was astonished. I had no idea the little things cost so much.

"There's the trained nurse for your wife," he went on, "at $25.00 a week for four weeks; and then the trained nurse for your baby, at $15.00 a week for forty-eight weeks; that makes $820.00. Then the doctor's bills, the clothes and so on--with the certified milk--easily take up the rest."

"Isn't fifteen dollars a week a good deal for a child's nurse?" I asked.

"What do you pay a good stenographer?" he demanded.

"Why, a special one gets $20.00," I admitted. "But that work needs training and experience."

"So does taking care of babies!" he cried triumphantly. "Don't try to save on babies, Morton; it's poor economy."

I liked his point of view, and admired his family extremely. His wife was one of those sympathetic appreciative women who so help a man in his work. But the prospects of my own marriage seemed remote. That was why I was so glad of a good wholesome companionable friend like Dodo.

We were so calmly intimate that I soon grew to discuss many of my ideas and plans with her. She was much interested in the figures given by my friend, and got me to set them all down for her. He had twice my salary, and not a cent left at the year's end; and they were not in "society" either. Five hundred dollars was allowed for his personal expenses, and the same for her; little enough to dress on nowadays, he had assured me, with all amusements, travel, books and periodicals, and dentist bills, included.

"I don't think it ought to cost so much," said Dodo.

She was a business woman, and followed the figures closely; and of course she appreciated the high views I held on the subject, and my self-denial, too.

I can't tell to this day how it happened; but before I knew it we were engaged. I was almost sorry, for a long engagement is a strain on both parties; but Dodo cheered me up; she said we were really no worse off than we were before, and in some ways better. At times I fully agreed with her.

So we drifted along for about a year, and then, after a good deal of distant discussion, we suddenly got married.

I don't recall now just why we so hastily concluded to do it; I seemed to be in a kind of dream; but anyway we did, and were absurdly happy about it, too.

"Don't be a Goose, dear boy!" she said. "It isn't wicked to be married. And we're quite old enough!"

"But we can't afford it--you know we can't," I said. This was while we were camping out on our honey-vacation.

"Mr. Morton Howland," said my wife; "don't you worry one bit about affording it. I want you to understand that you've married a business woman."

"But you've given up your position!" I cried, aghast. "Surely, you don't think of going back!"

"I've given up one position," she replied with calmness, "and taken another. And I mean to fill it. Now you go peacefully on earning what you did before, and leave the housekeeping business to me--will you, Dear?"

Naturally I had to; for I couldn't keep house; even if I so desired I didn't know how. But I had read so much and heard so much and seen so much of the difficulties of housekeeping for young married people, that I confess I was a good deal worried.

Toward the end of our trip I began to anticipate the burden of house-hunting.

"About where do you think we are going to live?" I tentatively inquired.

"At 384 Meter Avenue," she promptly answered. I nearly dropped the paddle (we were canoeing at the moment), I was so astonished.

"That's a good location--for cheap flats," I said slowly. "Do you mean to say you've rented one, all by yourself?"

She smiled comfortingly. Lovely teeth had my Dodo, strong and white and even, though not small.

"Not quite so bad as that, Dear," she answered, "but I've got the refusal. My friends the Scallens had it, and are moving out this Fall. It's a new building, they had it all papered very prettily, and if you like it we can move in as soon as they leave--say a week after moving time--it will be cheaper then. We'll look at it as soon as we return."

We did. It seemed suitable enough; pleasant, and cheaper than I had thought possible. Indeed, I demurred a little on the question of style, and accessibility to friends; but Dodo said the people who really cared for us would come, and the people who did not could easily be spared.

We had married so hastily, right on the verge of vacation time, that I had hardly given a thought to furnishing but Dodo seemed to know just where to go and what to get; at much less cost than I had imagined.

She produced $250.00 from her bank account, which she had been saving for years she said. I put up about the same; and we had that little flat as pretty and comfortable as any home I ever saw.

She set her foot down about pictures though. "Time enough for those things when we can afford it," she said, and we certainly could not afford it then.

Then was materialized from some foreign clime a neat, strong young woman to do our house-work, washing and all.

"She's an apprentice," said Dodo. "She is willing to learn housekeeping, and I am willing to teach her."

"How do you come to be so competent in house-work?" said I; "I thought you were a bookkeeper."

Then Dodo smiled her large bright smile. "Morton, dear," she said, "I will now tell you a Secret! I have always intended to marry, and, as far as possible, I learned the business. I am a business woman, you know."

She certainly did know her business. She kept the household accounts like--well, like what she was--an expert accountant. When she furnished the kitchen she installed a good reliable set of weights and measures. She weighed the ice and the bread, she measured the milk and the potatoes, and made firm, definite, accurate protests when things went wrong; even sending samples of queer cream to the Board of Health for analysis. What with my business stationery and her accurate figures our letters were strangely potent, and we were well supplied, while our friends sadly and tamely complained of imposture and extortion.

Her largest item of expense in furnishing was a first-class sewing machine, and a marvellous female figure, made to measure, which stood in a corner and served as a "cloak tree" when not in use.

"You don't propose to make your own clothes, surely?" said I when this headless object appeared.

"Some of 'em," she admitted, "you'll see. Of course I can't dress for society."

Now I had prepared myself very conscientiously to meet the storms and shallows of early married life, as I had read about them; I was bound I would not bring home anybody to dinner without telephoning, and was prepared to assure my wife verbally, at least twice a day, that I loved her. She anticipated me on the dinner business, however.

"Look here!" she said, leading me to the pantry, when it was filled to her liking, and she showed me a special corner all marked off and labelled "For Emergencies." There was a whole outfit of eatables and drinkables in glass and tin.

"Now do your worst!" she said triumphantly. "You can bring home six men in the middle of the night--and I'll feed them! But you mustn't do it two nights in succession, for I'd have to stock up again."

As to tears and nervousness and "did I love her," I was almost, sometimes, a bit disappointed in Dodo, she was so calm. She was happy, and I was happy, but it seemed to require no effort at all.

One morning I almost forgot, and left the elevator standing while I ran back to kiss her and say "I love you, dearest." She held me off from her with her two strong hands and laughed tenderly. "Dear boy!" she said, "I mean you shall."

I meditated on that all the way downtown.

She meant I should. Well, I did. And the next time one of my new-married friends circuitously asked for a bit of light on what was to him a dark and perplexing question, I suddenly felt very light-hearted about my domestic affairs. Somehow we hadn't any troubles at all. Dodo kept well; we lived very comfortably and it cost far less than I had anticipated.

"How did you know how to train a servant?" I asked my wife.

"Dear," said she, "I have admitted to you that I always intended to be married, when I found the man I could love and trust and honor." (Dodo overestimates my virtues, of course.)

"Lots of girls intend to marry," I interposed.

"Yes, I know they do," she agreed, "they want to love and he loved, but they don't learn their business! Now the business of house-work is not so abstruse nor so laborious, if you give your mind to it. I took an evening-course in domestic economy, read and studied some, and spent one vacation with an aunt of mine up in Vermont who 'does her own work.' The next vacation I did ours. I learned the trade in a small way."

We had a lovely time that first year. She dressed fairly well, but the smallness of her expense account was a standing marvel, owing to the machine and the Headless One.

"Did you take a course in dressmaking, too?" I inquired.

"Yes, in another vacation."

"You had the most industrious vacations of anyone I ever knew," said I, "and the most varied."

"I am no chicken, you see, my dear," was her cheerful reply, "and I like to work. You work, why shouldn't I?"

The only thing I had to criticize, if there was anything, was that Dodo wouldn't go to the theatre and things like that, as often as I wanted her to. She said frankly that we couldn't afford it, and why should I want to go out for amusement when we had such a happy home? So we stayed at home a good deal, made a few calls, and played cards together, and were very happy, of course.

All this time I was in more or less anxiety lest that thousand dollar baby should descend upon us before we were ready, for I had only six hundred in the bank now. Presently this dread event loomed awe-inspiringly on our horizon. I didn't say anything to Dodo about my fears, she must on no account be rendered anxious, but I lay awake nights and sometimes got up furtively and walked the floor in my room, thinking how I should raise the money.

She heard me one night. "Dear!" she called softly. "What are you doing? Is it burglars?"

I reassured her on that point and she promptly reassured me on the other, as soon as she had made me tell her what I was worrying about.

"Why, bless you, dear," she said, serenely, "you needn't give a thought to that. I've got money in the bank for my baby."

"I thought you spent all of it for the furnishings," said I.

"Oh, that was the Furnishing Money! Cuddle down here, or you'll get cold, and I'll tell you all about it."

So she explained in her calm strong cheerful way, with a little contented chuckle now and then, that she had always intended to be married.

"This is now no news," I exclaimed severely, "tell me something different."

"Well, in order to prepare for this Great Event," she went on, "I learned about housework, as you have seen. I saved money enough to furnish a small flat and put that in one bank. And I also anticipated this not Impossible Contingency and saved more money and put it in another bank!"

"Why two banks, if a mere man may inquire?"

"It is well," she replied sententiously, "not to have all one's eggs in one basket."

I lay still and meditated on this new revelation.

"Have you got a thousand dollars, if this Remote Relative may so far urge for information?"

"I have just that sum," she replied.

"And, not to be impertinent, have you nine other thousands of dollars in nine other banks for nine other not Impossible Contingencies?"

She shook her head with determination. "Nine is an Impossible Contingency," she replied. "No, I have but one thousand dollars in this bank. Now you be good, and continue to practice your business, into the details of which I do not press, and let me carry on the Baby Business, which is mine."

It was a great load off my mind, and I slept well from that time on.

So did Dodo. She kept well, busy, placid, and cheerful. Once, I came home in a state of real terror. I had been learning, from one of my friends, and from books, of the terrible experience which lay before her. She saw that I was unusually intense in my affection and constantly regarded her with tender anxiety. "What is the matter with you, Morton?" said she. "I'm--worried," I admitted. "I've been thinking--what if I should lose you! Oh Dodo! I'd rather have you than a thousand babies."

"I should think you would," said she calmly. "Now look here, Dear Boy! What are you worrying about? This is not an unusual enterprise I've embarked on; it's the plain course of nature, easily fulfilled by all manner of lady creatures! Don't you be afraid one bit, I'm not."

She wasn't. She kept her serene good cheer up to the last moment, had an efficient but inexpensive woman doctor, and presently was up again, still serene, with a Pink Person added to our family, of small size but of enormous importance.

Again I rather trembled for our peace and happiness, and mentally girded up my loins for wakeful nights of walking. No such troubles followed. We used separate rooms, and she kept the Pink Person in hers. Occasionally he made remarks in the night, but not for long. He was well, she was well--things went along very much as they did before.

I was "lost in wonder, love and praise" and especially in amazement at the continued cheapness of our living.

Suddenly a thought struck me. "Where's ths nurse?" I demanded.

"The nurse? Why she left long ago. I kept her only for the month."

"I mean the child's nurse," said I, "the fifteen dollar one."

"Oh--I'm the child's nurse," said Dodo.

"You!" said I. "Do you mean to say you take all the care of this child yourself?"

"Why, of course," said Dodo, "what's a mother for?"

"But--the time it takes," I protested, rather weakly.

"What do you expect me to do with my time, Morton?"

"Why, whatever you did before--This arrived."

"I will not have my son alluded to as 'This'!" said she severely. "Morton J. Hopkins, Jr., if you please. As to my time before? Why, I used it in preparing for time to come, of course. I have things ready for this youngster for three years ahead."

"How about the certified milk?" I asked.

Dodo smiled a superior smile; "I certify the milk," said she.

"Can you take care of the child and the house, too?"

"Bless you, Morton, 'the care' of a seven-room flat and a competent servant does not take more than an hour a day. And I market while I'm out with the baby.

"Do you mean to say you are going to push the perambulator yourself?"

"Why not?" she asked a little sharply, "surely a mother need not be ashamed of the company of her own child."

"But you'll be taken for a nurse--"

"I am a nurse! And proud of it!"

I gazed at her in my third access of deep amazement. "Do you mean to say that you took lessons in child culture, too?"

"Too? Why, I took lessons in child culture first of all. How often must I tell you, Morton, that I always intended to be married! Being married involves, to my mind, motherhood, that is what it is for! So naturally I prepared myself for the work I meant to do. I am a business woman, Morton, and this is my business."

*

That was twenty years ago. We have five children. Morton, Jr., is in college. So is Dorothea second. Dodo means to put them all through, she says. My salary has increased, but not so fast as prices, and neither of them so fast as my family. None of those babies cost a thousand dollars the first year though, nor five hundred thereafter; Dodo's thousand held out for the lot. We moved to a home in the suburbs, of course; that was only fair to the children. I live within my income always--we have but one servant still, and the children are all taught housework in the good old way. None of my friends has as devoted, as vigorous and--and--as successful a wife as I have. She is the incarnate spirit of all the Housewives and House-mothers of history and fiction. The only thing I miss in her--if I must own to missing anything--is companionship and sympathy outside of household affairs. My newspaper work--which she always calls "my business"--has remained a business. The literary aspirations I once had were long since laid aside as impracticable. And the only thing I miss in life beyond my home is, well--as a matter of fact, I don't have any life beyond my home--except, of course, my business.

My friends are mostly co-commuters now. I couldn't keep up with the set I used to know. As my wife said, she could 't dress for society, and, visibly, she couldn't. We have few books, there isn't any margin for luxuries, she says; and of course we can't go to the plays and concerts in town. But these are unessentials--of course--as she says.

I am very proud of my home, my family, and my Amazing Dodo.

2705162